I am Joseph

First published in the UK by Bright Books, an imprint of Beacon Books

Beacon Books and Media Ltd, Earl Business Centre, Dowry Street, Oldham, OL8 2PF, UK.

www.beaconbooks.net

Cataloging-in-Publication record for this book is available from the British Library

ISBN 978-1-912356-82-9 Paperback
ISBN 978-1-912356-83-6 Ebook

Cover design and illustrations by Sarah Nesti Willard

I am Jösëph

LILLY S. MOHSEN

Illustrated by Sarah Nesti Willard

BRIGHT BOOKS

The story you are about to read is based on true events.

Prölögüe

It was a vision too good to be true…
And an experience too real to be just a dream…

The voices in his head drowned into utter silence while he stared at this incredibly magnificent scene. Suspended somewhere between the highest skies and the Earth, the young boy was hypnotised. Standing on the top of what seemed to be an invisible mountain, the air around him glimmered with a million colours he never knew existed, and the whole universe bundled together as if it was suddenly the end of time and he was the only one who had survived. Powered by a superior command, the sun, moon and eleven stars prostrated themselves before the young boy, like ethereal beings kneeling humbly to a renowned king. Little did he know, it was at this moment that the boy's fate was sealed, and from now on, nothing would ever be the same again…

Chaptër Önë

As the sun bathed the horizon, Joseph opened his eyes, still trapped in that hazy moment between dreams and reality. He had heard about it and perhaps had briefly experienced it once or twice, but never did he fully understand how a feeling of happiness could be so intense it made your heart smile… until today.

Joseph suddenly jumped out of bed, unable to contain his excitement any longer.

"Father! Oh father, you will never believe the dream I had last night!"

Young Joseph lived with his family in a large yet simple house in a city named Canaan, south of Palestine. The walls of the two-storey house were built of roughly carved blocks of stone, and the top roof was made out of wooden beams covered with layers of branches and smoothed down with clay. A flight of wooden stairs led to the second floor, which consisted of a number of simple bedrooms for the family members. Joseph's father, Jacob, was usually the first to wake up and the last to go to bed at night. He had a special seating area situated in the courtyard, where he sat to relax and meditate. Looking up, Jacob smiled as he watched his son Joseph fly down the ladder with excitement.

"Well, good morning, Joseph!" his father said with a loving smile. "Come sit next to me, young man, and tell me all about your dream."

Amidst the scent of fresh air and the joyful twittering of birds at the early hours of dawn, Jacob's old age seemed to blend with a delightful history of wisdom and insight. The grandson of Prophet Abraham, Jacob (also known as Israel) was a messenger of God too, and the proud father of twelve sons: Reuben, Simon, Levi, Judah, Issachar, Zebulon, Dan, Naphtali, Gad and Asher. His late wife, Rachel, gave Jacob his youngest two boys, Joseph and Benjamin, before passing away during labour. Even though his current wife, Leya, took care of all the boys and loved them as if they were her own, Jacob had a soft spot for his youngest two, and tried to compensate for the loss of their mother by showering them with extra love and affection.

"Good morning, dear father!" Joseph grinned happily after bowing to kiss Jacob's hand. "Oh, I had the most amazing dream ever, and it felt real too! I saw the sun, the moon and eleven stars, and they were all bowing down to me."

Jacob's face lit up and his eyes glittered with tears of joy. Lost for words, he reached out and wrapped his arms around his son in a warm, protective embrace. He was suddenly overpowered with a captivating urge to shield him. Given his insight and perception, Jacob immediately foresaw the interpretation of his son's dream to be a sign of a bright future full of glory. Deciphering and translating visions was a talent that ran in the family, from one generation to the next. Not that Jacob was waiting for a dream to enhance the high hopes he had for his son. He knew Joseph would grow up to be legendary; it was a deeply rooted conviction planted in Jacob's heart since the blessed day his son was born…

***

It had been a harsh season of prolonged drought in the city of Harran back in Mesopotamia, and the people were desperately praying to their idol gods for mercy. They camped outside the temples day and night, sacrificing animals and bearing gifts, hoping the gods would finally release some much needed rain. Jacob was saddened by his own people's disbelief in the One and Only God, and made it his sole mission to guide them back to the right path. The priests were enraged by Jacob's ideas. Had he not been the nephew and son-in-law of Harran's esteemed governor, they would have thrown Jacob in the fire a long time ago, the same way they did with anyone audacious enough to insult their gods! They continuously blamed the messenger of God for the drought, saying the idols were angry at the whole city because of his blasphemy.

Jacob was not deterred, even now, with people throwing snide remarks his way while his beautiful wife Rachel was having difficulty during labour after more than ten years of waiting for a child together.

"The gods are punishing you, Jacob. Your wife has been in and out of consciousness for days. The idol gods are tormenting you slowly before they take your beloved Rachel and her baby away forever!" the priests of the temple gloated.

The townspeople waited for Rachel's death, an ultimate sign of the gods' wrath, but the Lord listened to

Jacob's supplications instead. He saved Rachel, the love of his life, and granted them a beautiful baby boy whom they named Joseph. That same night, the rain poured down, washing away the drought and the doubts people had. A whole city of disbelievers denounced their idols overnight and woke up to a new era of faith in the Lord and His chosen messenger.

Jacob doted on his new baby boy. He was a living reminder of God's miracles and blessings. Jacob already had ten older sons, and the brothers were starting to feel a tinge of jealousy towards Joseph, seeing how their father coddled him, and was always in high spirits when he was around. They all competed to win his affection, trying to impress Jacob the best way they knew how.

"Father, look at me!" Simon called out. "I can carry this huge rock all by myself."

Jacob was sitting in the yard with baby Joseph propped on his lap. He smiled at his sons as he watched them play and wrestle. They were all growing up so fast.

"I'll knock any one of you down with one punch," Judah boasted proudly. "I'm the strongest one in the family and will surely be father's successor someday."

"I'm the eldest. Don't you think that makes me the most eligible son for prophecy?" Reuben asked, already certain of the answer. The brothers argued and debated until Jacob finally decided to interfere.

"God will choose the most righteous and pious amongst you to be my heir. God looks at people's hearts, not their strength or status," Jacob said.

"So you mean instead of having one of your eldest sons carry on your legacy, God might choose this little baby to be the one?" Zebulon asked sarcastically.

"Perhaps. Who knows?" Jacob bent down to kiss little Joseph's soft cheek.

"Sometimes it seems you love Joseph more than us, father," Gad said sadly.

"Why? Because I let him sit on my lap? I did the same with all of you. But now you've grown up and become too big and strong," Jacob laughed.

Five years later Rachel was pregnant again and it brought even more happiness to the prophet's heart. She was such a beautiful, loving wife and a soft, caring mother. This time her difficult pregnancy was taking a toll on her health, especially during their long trip to Palestine after Jacob announced it was time to move to Canaan. Her frail body couldn't take the pain of labour.

"Hang in there, Rachel! It won't be long now," her sister Leya, Jacob's other wife, said. She used a small cloth to wipe the sweat off Rachel's forehead, her face pale with sorrow.

"My time has come, Leya. It's the Great Lord's will," Rachel panted. "Promise me you'll take care of my children and love them as your own…"

She gave Jacob his last gift, a baby boy named Benjamin, before taking her final breath, and taking away with her a piece of her husband's heart.

"Mommy! Nooooo!" Joseph cried, hugging Rachel's corpse. He watched them bury his mother's body under the dust with his new baby brother screaming at the top of his lungs, as if he felt his arrival had caused his mother's death and brought a cold, harsh destiny of being forever deprived of her warmth and love.

***

"Hmm, eleven stars, the sun and the moon." Joseph squinted his eyes and smiled at his father. "You're an expert in translating dreams. What do you think this one means?"

A serious look of concern had somehow replaced the happiness in Jacob's eyes like a gloomy cloud that blocked the shining rays of the morning sun.

"What's wrong, father?" Joseph asked.

"Did you mention this dream to any of your brothers?" Jacob asked in an apprehensive tone.

"No, not yet. You're the first one I wanted to tell."

Joseph and his father had a special bond engraved with love and respect. He was the first person Joseph ran to when he had something to share. His father was his mentor and his friend, for he understood Joseph better than anyone else. He took Joseph's thoughts and dreams seriously, and took the time to explain and teach him about life. No father ever loved his son the way Jacob loved Joseph. He was the light of his whole life, and the soothing balm that eased his pain. At just ten years of age, Joseph was a sight for sore eyes. He had his mother's stunning beauty. His dark hair was long and soft, his eyes deep like the ocean, and his face glowed with translucent light. He had the most charming looks a young boy could possibly ever possess and the brightest smile like an angel from heaven. Little Joseph was every parent's dream child: gentle, caring and obedient. He was smart, cheerful and always willing to offer a helping hand. Out of all of Jacob's sons, Joseph was his favourite by far, and it didn't take much for anyone around to notice it.

"Please don't mention this dream to your brothers," Jacob warned Joseph. "I'm scared they may hurt you or plot against you. The devil whispers evil thoughts to humans, my son, and makes good people do very bad things. Satan is man's mortal enemy!"

As much as he would have loved to deny it, Joseph couldn't help but recall his elder brothers' suppressed hatred towards him. Their jealousy wrapped around him like cold bars of steel. It always seemed like Joseph and Benjamin were on one side and his elder ten brothers were on the other. Perhaps their envy stemmed from the fact that their father was overly protective of the youngest two boys. He had overheard their spiteful comments many times before, but it did not change the way he felt about his brothers. He loved them very much, and wanted nothing more than for them to love him back.

"The Lord will choose you, Joseph. He will teach you and bless you with His favours, the same way He blessed your fathers Abraham and Isaac before you. Your Lord is All-Knowing and All-Wise," Jacob said.

"You told me the story of Adam and Eve, and how the devil made them disobey the Lord, causing them to descend from Paradise. Why does the devil hate humans so much?" Joseph asked.

"It's because Satan was jealous of Adam, for the Lord honoured humans over all His other creations," Jacob said. "Since that time, jealousy has been one of the main roots of all evil. It's the poisonous weapon the devil uses to come between even the closest of family members and friends. Never let jealousy or conceit enter your heart, Joseph, for it will stain its purity beyond repair."

The young boy paused for a minute to absorb his father's insinuations. Was he really the chosen one? Had his father known this all along and was that why he

favoured Joseph the most? His father always spoke about people's natural instincts, and evil wasn't one of them. Would telling his brothers about his glorious dream make them feel less about themselves and perhaps cause them to conspire against him? There definitely was a reason behind Jacob's warning to keep this vision a secret. Perhaps some blessings weren't meant to be shared, Joseph concluded, especially if they hadn't come true yet.

Joseph kissed his father's hand again and excused himself to go wash up before breakfast. The explanations and mysteries of their conversation were still echoing in his head when his brother Benjamin came out of nowhere to interrupt his thought.

"I am mad at you!" Benjamin said, with his arms crossed and pouted lips.

"Hey there, little fellow." Joseph lifted his brother up playfully. "Good morning to you, too!"

"No! Put me down. I'm mad at you!"

"You're mad at *me*?" Joseph gasped in feigned disbelief. "Oh my God, what did I do to your majesty?"

"I woke up and you were not there."

"Well, I do apologise for that, but I needed to talk to father before everyone else woke up. Now if you'll excuse me, I need to go prepare a smiley-face apple pie for King Benjamin while he goes to wash up."

"You're the best brother in the whole wide world!" Benjamin called, whilst scurrying away happily.

A little while later, the ten older brothers all came back home for a short break, sweating and mumbling grumpily about having to go to work before sunrise. It was the ploughing season again, and that required the hardest work of all. It usually took a whole day of constant labour, involving cutting, lifting and turning soil to prepare for the new seedbeds. Leya was sitting by the small clay oven, her face flushed red from its heat, handing out fresh hot baked bread. Joseph helped put some pots of food on the ground and ran outside to fill the water vessels for his tired brothers who had already started devouring their breakfast.

"Good morning. Are you guys hungry, too?" He greeted and fed the sheep gathered around him, then pulled out the bucket from the well. A flimsy wooden fence sequestered the courtyard where all the animals lived. Joseph took a minute to stare at the open desert stretched out before him. The sand reflected the golden shimmer of the sun. It was all very pure and peaceful, just like this young boy's heart...

"How about you send Joseph with us today to help out in the field, father?" Gad asked, chewing on a piece of celery.

"He has his chores to finish here," Jacob replied firmly, "and you know I don't allow him or Benjamin out of the house anyway. They're still too young to work in the fields."

"His hands are probably too delicate and precious to touch the soil!" Simon mumbled under his breath.

"What did you say, son?" Jacob asked.

"Nothing, father! I totally agree with you. Farming needs strong arms and well-built bodies. Joseph and Benjamin are still children—they can't handle that kind of harsh work," Gad added hastily.

"Your brothers are young men now, Gad! I just prefer they stay here to take care of your mother's needs and mine," Jacob said calmly.

"As you wish, father," Reuben, the eldest son, said before getting up to leave. "We will see you at dinner."

"May the Lord give you more strength and patience, my sons," Jacob smiled. "Have a good day."

Naturally, after being informed of Joseph's future grand status through his blessed vision, Jacob fussed over his young son a little more. He was truly unable to part from Joseph for even the shortest period of time. Jacob's mixed emotions of worry, honour and affection enveloped his young boy like a magical shield of love. Just when the eldest brothers thought Jacob could not possibly love Joseph any more, he did, and it was becoming too much for the elder sons to ignore.

One evening, while the ten brothers worked in the fields, the subject of their father's overprotection and deep love for Joseph came up as usual.

"What does our father see in him?" Levi asked the rest as he shoveled away more mud.

"Maybe it's because he's so handsome," Zebulon snarled with disgust. "Are boys even supposed to be that pretty?!"

"I don't think it's his looks that makes father favour Joseph the most," Judah said while digging out narrow water canals. "I think it's because he's so ridiculously pleasant all the time. Boys his age should be wild and loud and climbing up walls just to drive everyone crazy. Remember how we were when we were younger?" he laughed.

"Father insists he loves us all the same and treats us equally. He just feels sorry for Joseph and Benjamin. His sympathy shouldn't bother us this much," Levi explained.

"Oh that's right! We do all the work, plant the crops, herd the sheep, clean the animals' filth and basically do all the heavy lifting. Joseph helps out with some simple house chores, sits next to father all night looking pretty, and gets all the admiration. Sounds fair, Levi! I wonder what we are all so upset about!" Judah said, his words dripping with sarcasm and disdain.

"We're a group of strong, virile men. Practically a clan of our own, powerful enough to rule this city. We should be father's pride and joy. And yet he treats this orphan child as if he was the future leader. He has no problem with us being away all day, but Joseph? Oh, God forbid he should step out of the house lest he scrape his precious knee or get mud on his pretty face! I'm telling you, father's mind is clearly slipping," Reuben commented rudely.

"Don't you dare insult our father! He is a Prophet of God!" Levi yelled at his eldest brother, while the others held him back to prevent a huge fight from starting.

"This is all Joseph's fault," Gad said. "He's the reason we're always arguing lately. Sometimes I wish he never existed. Things would be far less complicated."

"Just imagine if there was no Mr. Perfect in our lives?" Naphtali said. "I bet our father would have all the time and love in the world for us."

"We are a group of strong, undefeatable men, and yet he chooses that little youngster over us! Turns out our father isn't that wise after all, is he?" Reuben said.

"You know you had a point there before," Dan pointed to Naphtali, who had spoken earlier. "Imagine if Joseph suddenly disappeared from our lives!"

"That would be a dream come true. If only we had a magic wand." Issachar shared his secret wish while drawing circles on the ground with a twig.

"We don't need a magic wand. We just need a plan."

"What kind of plan?" the rest asked curiously.

"You know how people say, 'out of sight, out of mind'? That's exactly what we need. We need to remove Joseph from the picture so our father will eventually forget about him and focus on us," Judah said with an evil twinkle in his eyes.

"What are you getting at, Judah?" Reuben asked.

Clenching his jaw in anger, Judah replied spitefully, "We can kill him…"

Silence haunted the crop field like a dark ghost of lethal smoke. The brothers paused, pondering on the thought in their minds, and what the others were thinking. Joseph dying was the answer to all their problems, but actually murdering their little brother with their own hands was a tad too evil, wasn't it?

Wasn't it…?

Chaptër Twö

"We can *kill* him," Judah stressed the words, looking his nine brothers in the eyes.

"You can't be serious. How can you even suggest such a thing? Have you lost your mind?" Levi asked.

"I haven't lost my mind, Levi. In fact, I'm brave enough to voice the thoughts on *all* your minds!" Judah replied.

"We can't kill Joseph. We are the noble sons of Israel, the Prophet of God. Out of all people, we know how grave of a sin it is to murder an innocent soul," Reuben said.

"You think Joseph is innocent?" Judah scoffed. "He's a manipulative thief! He stole father's heart and stole our joy with it. He stole our chances of becoming father's heirs and this town's future leaders. He even stole our mother's love. He stole our whole identities! How great of a sin is that, Reuben? How come he gets to walk free?"

"Judah is right... Joseph may have fooled father, but he hasn't fooled the rest of us. Remember what happened a couple of years ago? Must I remind you what else he stole...?"

***

17

"My condolences, Messenger of God. I'm so sorry for your loss. I know how much you loved Rachel and how great of a mother she was," Joseph's aunt said sadly.

"Thank you, sister. May God bestow His mercy and patience on all of us," Jacob replied, his head resting on the trunk of a palm tree next to his beloved wife's grave.

The whole family had just moved to Canaan, where Jacob's sister lived. The city leaders all came to pay their respects, and vowed to obey his Lord's commands, the same way they took the pledge of monotheism with his father, Prophet Isaac. They offered him a place to stay close to his sister's house, who was overjoyed to finally meet her nephews, especially Joseph, whom she instantly fell in love with.

"I want to help. With her sister's passing, Leya must be extremely overwhelmed taking care of twelve children. It's too much for her. Baby Benjamin alone is a handful at this age. Would you allow me the honour of raising Joseph in my house for a while?"

"I appreciate your offer, sister, but I'm afraid I will have to refuse. My heart is attached to Joseph in a way I can't explain; it would be impossible for me to give him up. Besides, I promised Rachel I would take care of him."

"It's only for a couple of months, till you settle down in Canaan and Leya regains her strength after the mourning period. Please, Jacob. I promise I will guard Joseph with my life. You know I don't have any children of my own, and your son captivated my heart at first sight. Please accept my request. It would serve everybody well."

After Jacob's reluctant approval, five-year-old Joseph moved to his aunt's house, and filled her life with joy.

She fed him, bathed him and told him bedtime stories. She taught him everything she knew and made sure he was well groomed and perfectly dressed at all times. Jacob came to visit every day, which aggravated his sons a lot. They were finally relieved to get rid of the little boy, only to find their father spending more time with him at his sister's house. One day, while Joseph was playing hide and seek with some of the kids from the neighbourhood, he suddenly went missing, and his aunt panicked, looking for him everywhere. Even though they finally found him later, Jacob insisted he take his son home.

"You don't trust me with him anymore?" the aunt asked sadly.

"Of course I do. I just wouldn't forgive myself if something happened to him. Besides, Benjamin is older now, and I would like for the brothers to grow up together." Jacob explained.

"Give me a couple of days to adjust. Giving Joseph back will probably be the hardest thing I will ever have to do in my life. It's like snatching my heart out of my chest," his aunt cried.

Joseph wasn't in a hurry to leave either. His aunt was kind and caring, and she was very attached to him. His leaving would surely cause her a lot of pain.

"So you don't mind staying with me a while longer?" his aunt asked hopefully.

"Not at all, I love it here! But what about father?" little Joseph asked.

"Don't worry about him. I have a plan to keep you here, but I will need your help to make it work."

The next morning, the aunt took Joseph back to his family's house, then returned the same evening looking very distressed. She told Jacob she had lost their father Isaac's belt. She looked everywhere but couldn't find it, and insinuated that perhaps his son had taken it.

"Joseph is not a thief!" Jacob was very offended.

"He's young, he doesn't understand it's a big sin to steal. Maybe he thought I gave it to him. Do you mind if I search him?" she asked.

The members of the family and some of the neighbours gathered around to watch how this would all end.

"This is ridiculous! Is this some kind of ploy to keep Joseph in your house?" Jacob asked indignantly when the belt was found around the child's waist.

"I have no tricks up my sleeve, dear brother," the aunt lied. "I'm only retrieving what is rightfully mine. And since Joseph stole my belt, according to the great Canaanite laws, I'm entitled to enslave him for four years."

"Enslave him? He's a child for God's sake! You can't do this to us!" Leya exploded.

"I believe I can. Rules are rules. But don't worry, brother, I promise I'll treat Joseph well," the aunt said. She took Joseph home, believing her guilt was a small price to pay for the happiness this young boy gave her. It was either this trick or dying from the heartache of parting with Joseph.

A couple more years passed, and Joseph was sad to see his aunt getting older and weaker. He stayed by her side, taking care of her and cheering her up with interesting limericks. But sickness overcame her and the whole family gathered by her deathbed to bid her a final farewell, while Joseph held her hand and sobbed silently.

"I'm scared, Jacob!" the aunt cried after coughing a handful of blood into a handkerchief.

"I know, sister. Death can be scary, but we are all guests in this world and will all die one day, too," Jacob said sadly.

"That's not why I'm scared. I'm afraid to meet God after what I've done. I'm so grateful He brought you all here so I can confess my sin and die with a clear conscience. Oh brother, please forgive me."

She told them the truth about the belt and how she did it because she loved Joseph and wasn't ready to let him go. Joseph never stole anything and he was certainly nobody's slave. She took a breath of relief and closed her eyes for the last time, leaving Joseph to relive the heartaching loss of his mother yet again.

***

"I always doubted that confession. She only said it to exonerate her favourite nephew. She didn't want Joseph to live in shame after she's gone," Asher said.

"That's neither here nor there. Even if Joseph had committed that crime, it still doesn't justify murdering him!" Levi insisted.

"Do you have a better suggestion? Or have you made peace with the fact this little spoiled boy will become our leader one day? Man up, Levi! We're taking matters into our own hands and preventing father from making a grave mistake."

"I agree with Levi," Reuben, the eldest of the brothers, reasoned quickly. "We don't have to kill Joseph; we can throw him in a well far from here. Maybe someone will find him and take him away forever."

"Yes, that sounds like a plan! Let's just get rid of him," they all agreed. "But how will we ever get him alone? Father never lets Joseph out of his sight!"

The ten brothers wasted no time in hatching out the perfect plot. They carefully deliberated on how to convince their father to let Joseph out of the house, and where they'd take their young brother when Jacob finally approved. They needed an alibi or a reasonable explanation to give their father after they got rid of Joseph and came home without him. As they ploughed the farm, Satan sowed the seeds of hatred and betrayal in their hearts. The blood boiled in their veins and feelings of guilt and remorse evaporated along with their sound judgments. Details were discussed and tweaked to perfection, and the more they visualised it, the more desperate they became for their dream to come true.

"Remember, we are doing this for a greater cause," Reuben reassured the rest of them on the way home. "We will ask God to forgive us later, and resume our lives as good people. Trust me, we *will* become better people after Joseph is gone."

Jealousy...

It's the one feeling no one wants to admit, and everyone tries to justify.

It's the one feeling that eats hearts alive, corrupts souls, and makes good people do very bad things...

That same night, when the whole family finished having dinner and the two younger boys went to sleep, the ten older brothers sat their father down to carry out the first step of the plan.

"It's always a pleasure to spend some quality time

with my boys," Jacob smiled. "It's been a long time since we all sat together and had a nice talk."

"We sort of had a question to ask you, father," Gad said. "My brothers and I were wondering why you never let Joseph go out with us every now and then? He's young and vibrant, he needs some 'outdoor' time to play and enjoy himself."

Jacob remained silent for a long time. He looked Gad in the eyes, and saw him quickly look away with agitation. For some reason Jacob couldn't explain, his son's seemingly light comment gave him a heavy heart.

"Let Joseph go out with us tomorrow, father," Levi interrupted Jacob's thoughts abruptly. "The weather at this time of year is absolutely amazing. It would do his health good to get some fresh air."

"Joseph has a lot of work to do in the house," Jacob frowned. "Maybe some other day."

"Benjamin can stay and help out with that," Issachar suggested. "We are having a nice picnic in the desert tomorrow, and I'm sure Joseph would love to join us."

"What's the matter, father? Don't you trust us with our own brother?" Asher asked, putting Jacob on the spot.

"That's not the point. I'm just so used to Joseph being around, it will make me very sad to see him go," Jacob admitted. "You want to take him out in the wilderness! What if a wolf attacks him?"

"You think we'd let that happen?" Reuben asked, pretending to be offended by the insinuation. "Or are you suggesting we are a bunch of idiots who can't even protect our own brother? We are a group of strong, undefeatable men, father! We will definitely take care of Joseph and watch him like hawks. I only want our brother to have some fun for a couple of hours. Give me one good reason why he can't?"

"Let me think about it, son." Jacob was reluctantly giving in to their persistence.

"There's nothing to think about, my dear father," Asher faked a reassuring smile. "Give us this chance to make our little brother happy, will you?"

It was awkward for Jacob to keep making excuses for why he didn't want Joseph to go out with them to play. Reuben was right, young boys should be able to enjoy outdoor activities every once in a while. Jacob loved his sons, and rejecting their kind offer might build a wall between them in the future. They gave their solemn word they'd take good care of Joseph and bring him back safe and sound. Perhaps it was time to loosen his grip on his young son and let him out into the real world. At least just this one time, Jacob convinced himself, despite the voice in his heart urging him not to.

"I guess Joseph can go out with you, as long as you promise to take good care of him," their father sighed before wishing them a good night.

"Oh, we definitely will," Levi whispered sarcastically as he watched his father walk away.

**

Jacob hardly slept all night, tossing and turning in bed with grave uneasiness. Finally surrendering to his insomnia, the old man went to sit by the window, staring at the silver moon that always kept him company when sleep abandoned him. He wondered how sincere his older sons were in wanting Joseph to enjoy his time with them. Why now? Did someone overhear his conversation with Joseph about his beautiful vision? Was the heeding voice of his heart correct? Was he making the right decision letting him go when he knew his sons well, and knew how Satan could easily toy with their arrogant, jealous hearts?

"What's wrong, dear?" his wife Leya asked in a sleepy voice.

"Nothing. I just have a lot on my mind," Jacob replied wearily.

"Is this about Joseph going out with his brothers tomorrow?"

"I know you think I'm overly protective of him and Benjamin, but I have my reasons, Leya!"

"I never said that. I actually love how you're so caring and tender with your sons, especially the younger ones who need it the most. I've lived the most blessed and happiest years of my life with you, Jacob," his wife said softly. "I know your heart is drawn to Joseph the most, and I don't blame you. That boy is like an angel sent from above! Yet you treat us all with love, fairness and respect and for that I'll forever be grateful."

"You and my boys are so dear to me. It would break my heart if anything bad happened to any one of you, God forbid! Especially Joseph. He's still so young and inexperienced. Do you think I shouldn't let him go out tomorrow?"

"I trust your judgement, Jacob, but you need to remember that Joseph is a child. He needs to play and run around like all the other children. He will have ten men guarding him alone. Have faith that nothing will happen to him against the Lord's will," she reasoned.

"You're right, Leya. Nothing happens against the Lord's will…"

***

"For real?" Joseph jumped up happily, unable to contain his excitement when he heard the news in the morning. "My brothers want me to join them for a picnic? Oh my God, they're the best brothers ever!"

"Joseph, I'll let you go only if you give me a man's word," Jacob went down to his knees to be at eye level with his beloved son. "I need you to promise me that you'll take care of yourself, and never stay out of your brothers' sight, not even for a second."

"I promise, father."

"Today, a whole new phase of your life will start. You're going out into the real world without me for the first time. Whatever happens, I know you'll handle it well and stay strong. You're my son, Joseph, and I know I taught you well."

"Don't worry about me, father. I'll make you proud."

Joseph ran to change his clothes before his father could change his mind. His heart was dancing inside his chest, and he couldn't stop smiling. His brothers actually requested he join them for an all-boys picnic! How great was that?

"Joseph?" Benjamin sneaked into his room while everyone was busy getting ready to leave. "Are you really going with them?" he asked sadly.

"Yes, Benjamin. You know I'd love for you to join us too," Joseph said in a warm, gentle tone, "but we can't leave father alone now, can we? He needs a man in the house with him!"

Benjamin lowered his head sadly, trying to hold back his tears.

"I promise you, next time I'll stay and you can go. I'll just go check out the place first, see if it's good enough for King Benjamin! Deal?"

"Don't go, Joseph. Please don't leave."

Joseph couldn't handle seeing his little brother so sad. He hugged Benjamin warmly and assured him he wouldn't be long. Benjamin was still young; he wouldn't understand Joseph's need to bond with the rest of his brothers and strengthen the unity of the family. He always knew his brothers would come around and let go of their hatred towards him, and that day was finally here.

"You've never left me before, Joseph. We do everything together. And now you're leaving and I can't stay here without you," Benjamin cried.

"You make it sound like I'm leaving forever," Joseph laughed. "It's just a couple of hours while you finish your chores. I promise I'll tell you an extra bedtime story tonight, and tell you all about the picnic too."

"You didn't even have time to prepare my special milk drink this morning," Benjamin sniffled.

"It's because I know that in three seconds, Mother Leya will open the door and bring you your drink and some dates too!" Joseph winked.

"Benjamin?" Leya walked in holding a small tray. "I got you your favourite drink and some sweet dates. Would you like to sit with me in the garden after your brothers leave?"

"Sure, Mother Leya! I'll say goodbye to Joseph and come join you right away," Benjamin replied politely.

"Very well then," Leya said, "I'll be downstairs if anybody needs me. Have a wonderful time with your big brothers, Joseph."

"Thank you, Mother Leya," Joseph kissed her happily.

"Oh my God!" Benjamin exclaimed when Leya left. "How did you know what food she was bringing?"

"It's just a little talent I have." Joseph bowed in a dramatic manner before hugging his brother again. "Oh Ben... I miss you already."

It was time to go. The young men were all geared up to leave, with straw baskets bearing drinks and snacks Leya made for the picnic.

"Come on, Joseph. We are all waiting for you!" he heard Asher call from downstairs.

"I'll be right there!" Joseph shouted back excitedly.

"Take care of our father for me, Benjamin," Joseph said softly.

"Take care of yourself for us, Joseph," Benjamin wept silently, as he bid his beloved brother farewell.

Forming a narrow strip between the Jordanian desert and the Mediterranean Sea, the city of Canaan boasted a spectacular location, and yet in return, suffered from constant weather fluctuations and times of drought. Feeling the summer heat run through his soft hair, Joseph marvelled at the alleys and neighbourhood passageways, smiling happily every time a passer-by greeted his brothers with respect. Jacob's sons were obviously highly valued in their community. Prancing through the crowds on their camels, shooing the herd of sheep all the way out to the open desert, Joseph's heart was filled with immense gratification. He was genuinely proud to be part of this family. He felt safe and protected amongst his strong, grown-up brothers. At the mark of his first jaunt away from home he was confident this day was the start of a whole new beginning. Together, hand in hand, they would help carry the Prophet's legacy and make this world a much better place.

The ten brothers were awfully silent during the trip to their destination. Joseph tried to make jokes and start a conversation but no one seemed interested. After dismounting their rides, they just kept walking, each shrouded in a dark cloud of thought. They looked tense and anxious, like they were carrying invisible loads on their backs. Were they maybe lost and too proud to admit it? Joseph wondered as he followed in their footsteps.

"Are we there yet?" Joseph finally asked after what seemed like a hundred hours of walking deep into the desert. He couldn't wait to get there and start the fun. He heard his brothers tell their father they were going to play all kinds of different games. Maybe hide and seek! He beamed happily.

"We are almost there, pretty face!" Gad sneered at him with a spark of evil in his eyes. If Joseph had noticed his tone, he never gave it much attention. He was used to their sarcasm every now and then, and he somehow learnt never to let it bother him. It was nice of them to let him tag along, and that was enough improvement for now.

They finally reached an isolated well in the middle of nowhere. It was a vast space of yellow shabbiness, with nothing and no one in sight. So much for dressing up, Joseph smiled to himself. Well, he didn't know what to expect, and he wanted to look great for his first outing with his brothers.

"Anyone up for a drink?" Dan asked, sticking his head inside the well to examine the depth of it. They couldn't figure out the distance downwards last night when they came to inspect the well, since it was too dark. But now, standing here in the bright daylight, he couldn't even see the bottom of it.

Perfect!

"You guys are so lucky to know your way around with so much ease," Joseph marvelled at his big brothers. "I don't think I can find my way back home, not in a million years."

"That's the whole point, princess!" hissed Levi.

"Don't call me that, please," Joseph replied politely. "I'm a man!"

"Yeah? Show us how much of a man you are! Go down that well and get us some water," Simon mocked him nastily.

"I'll need a bucket and a rope," Joseph replied, confused at the sudden aggression.

"The little prince needs a golden bucket, doesn't he?" Dan sneered as he shoved his little brother hard, while the others laughed.

"I wonder what it's like at the bottom of this deep well?" Naphtali sniggered. "It must be scary down there, huh?"

"Maybe you'll find some nice corpses inside to keep you company, pretty face!" Issachar laughed. "Or maybe you'll make friends with the snakes and scorpions. You love all kinds of animals, right?"

"Why are you all being so mean to me?" Joseph

asked, wanting to scream. "What did I ever do to you?"

"Just that innocent look of yours is downright disgusting," Zebulon shoved him again, a lot harder this time.

"Stop it! I don't want a picnic anymore," Joseph cried out, "I want to go home, please."

"Shut it!" Gad slapped the young boy on the face. "You may have tricked our father, but you can't deceive us with your fake decency."

"What are you talking about?" Joseph held a palm to his burning cheek from the hard slap, his eyes wide and red with confusion and hurt.

"Shut your mouth, you little piece of garbage. I'm glad I will never have to hear your squeaky annoying voice again!" Judah grabbed his little brother by his shirt and lifted him up from the ground till he almost choked. He then flung him to Dan who punched him hard in the face, causing his nose to bleed. They all circled around the little mortified boy like a pack of wolves, shoving and tossing him back and forth.

"Father! Someone help me!" Joseph cried out, his heart pounding louder than his own screams.

"I said SHUT IT!" Judah dragged his little brother by his hair, then threw him on the hot, rough ground. The brothers all cramped in to take their turns in kicking Joseph with their feet, and he buried his head in the dust to protect his face.

"Please stop! Please! What did I do?"

"I can kill you right now." Judah suddenly took out a sharp knife and put it to his terrified brother's throat.

"That's enough, Judah. Let's stick to what we agreed on and get this over with," Reuben said. He grabbed

Joseph by his clothes and pulled him up to his feet. His eyes and mouth were filled with sand and dust, he could hardly breathe and his whole body, covered in bloody bruises, trembled uncontrollably. He coughed and gasped for air, thanking his eldest brother for putting an end to his torture.

"We were only getting started." Reuben's words echoed inside Joseph like a shattering earthquake, making his legs weaken.

Like a cue to attack, and before the little boy could respond, Gad grabbed Joseph's arms tightly and put them above his head, then Dan and Asher quickly stripped him of his shirt.

Joseph tried to struggle as they brutally strangled him and tied a big rope around his waist and carried him to the brim of the dark well. He tried to wiggle out of their fierce grips, but there were too many of them, and he was just a little boy. His heart was pounding; he thought it would burst from the shock and fear he felt when he took a glimpse of how deep and dark the well was. The looks on his brothers' faces told him it was not an act or a sick game. It was a plot against him, just like his father Jacob had speculated. Or perhaps a nightmare that he'd soon wake up from…

"I'm scared, Reuben. Please. I'll do anything you want. Please don't leave me here!" Joseph clenched tight at his eldest brother's neck. "You promised father you'd take care of me! Remember? Reuben! Look at me. You promised father…"

"What the hell are you waiting for?" Reuben yanked his arms away and yelled at the rest of them. "Throw him over and let's get out of here!"

"No, please!" Joseph screamed. "Why? What did I do?"

The brothers dangled him down the well before completely letting go of the rope. They heard the little boy's screams fade away the further he descended into its infinite darkness. He fell down the long void of the well's depth till he thrashed into the water. It was a frozen sunken, moment trapped between reality and a dreadful dream, where the little boy reached the peak of horrifying fear and totally lost consciousness.

"Get his shirt!" Naphtali yelled. "Come on, let's go!"

Judah grabbed a sheep from the herd, held it in place with one elbow and slit its throat open angrily with his sharp knife. The rest of the brothers watched dumbfounded while Dan handed him Joseph's shirt to stain it with the dead animal's blood.

Their cold-hearted crime lurked in the hot forsaken desert, while the ten young men fled the scene, petrified at the enormity of what they had done. They felt their hearts spring up to their throats and their heads throb with extreme fear. They ran away from the memory of their betrayal, haunted by the painful look they saw in Joseph's eyes.

A rush of triumph shrouded in evil and self-disdain trailed behind the brothers as they prepared to go home and face their father. It was the last step, and perhaps the hardest of all…

"Let's wait," Asher stopped halfway home. "I think it's better to wait till nighttime comes. It will look like we took our time to search for Joseph before giving up."

"Yes, let's camp out here for a couple of hours," Reuben agreed, relieved at the suggested delay in schedule.

Panting and overwhelmed, they all sat down in the shade, sharing the food Leya had packed for the so-called 'picnic', and talking about everything else but the one thing they needed to discuss. They threw the leftovers to the crows surrounding their criminal gathering like moths around a blazing fire, ignoring the fact they never bothered to leave any food for their little brother.

"Do you think father will believe our story?" Asher finally asked after a long silence.

"The only way father will believe our story is if we believe it first!" Levi snapped. "And we do. Don't we, my dear brothers?"

"Yes, we do," they all agreed.

"Besides, it's possible someone already found Joseph and took him away to a better place. If you think about it, we never really committed any sin. It could be that we did him good, actually," Judah reasoned.

"Who are you kidding, Judah?" Levi scoffed. "That well is extremely deep and way off track. Who could possibly find him now? He'll probably starve to death before anyone realises he was even there!"

Another conflict surfaced between the jittery brothers, each one blaming and accusing the other till they all got tangled up in a fist fight. They didn't trust each other anymore after what had happened. The remorse and fear were building up inside their souls like hungry monsters, and this guilt-ridden violence was the only thing that helped numb the pain.

"Enough! That's the first and last time I want to hear about what really happened out there! You understand?" Reuben snapped in a threatening voice. "We will never, and I mean *never*, speak of the truth to anyone. Not even to ourselves! Am I making myself clear?"

Reuben peeled the brothers off each other to stop the ruckus. They each went to sit in a different place, alone with their thoughts, mentally practising the inevitable confrontation with their father, and hoping their eldest brother was right… That indeed it could all be over soon and they would all one day forget Joseph ever existed. As darkness veiled the night, the brothers dragged their feet home along with their lies, their mixed feelings clashing together like the high waves of the angry sea. They held their fire torches away from their lowered heads to conceal their shameful eyes. Dan trailed behind, gripping tight at the bloodstained shirt, the only proof they had to show for their false defence. They could see Jacob from afar, waiting outside the front yard for their arrival. He went down to the ground to prostrate in gratefulness to the Lord when he saw his sons approaching. They said they would be back before sunset, and he had been counting the seconds since then. But now Jacob could finally take a deep breath of relief; they were here now and that's all that really mattered.

He could tell his sons seemed tired. Their pace was slower than usual.

"What's wrong?" Jacob asked when he saw the looks on their faces, feeling a sudden thunderbolt strike his heart.

"Where is Joseph…?"

Chapter Three

The loud, hammering beats of the ten brothers' hearts vibrated like heavy drumming in suspense. It was hard to read the expression on their faces in the dim candlelight, but Jacob felt the anxiety through their silence and uneven breathing. He knew something terrible had happened. Sharp pins and needles pricked at the old man's skin as he waited for his sons to explain.

"Where is Joseph, Reuben?" Jacob asked his eldest son.

"Oh father! We left Joseph by our belongings and went racing. We didn't want him to fall or hurt himself," Reuben replied through his crocodile tears. "But by the time we came back…"

"What you feared has happened, father," Levi continued, believing his own lie. "A wolf ate poor little Joseph while we were gone!"

The ten brothers fell to their knees one by one, tears rolling down their faces, throwing dust on their heads and wailing loudly into the still, ominous night.

"But… I don't understand," Jacob stuttered. "You said you would take care of him."

"We did! But I guess we lost track of time when we went racing," Asher cried.

"This can't be true. No, no, it's not true," Jacob panicked, grabbing at each of his sons' cloaks. "Issachar! Dan! Naphtali! Tell me the truth!"

"You don't believe us, do you?" Dan cried out. "Even when we say the truth, you never believe us, father."

"We brought you his shirt as proof. Look! It's drenched in his blood. Oh, poor Joseph," Levi said.

Like a grand ship hit by a malicious storm, Jacob's heavy heart sunk his body down slowly. He held onto the arms of his chair to stop himself from falling to the ground.

Jacob stared back at the ten grown men, feeling like time had paused with an endless, merciless grip on his soul. The shocking news rang in his ears with a deafening high-pitched alarm sound. It took him a while to absorb what his sons were saying until he finally reached out his shaking hand to touch his beloved son's shirt, the tarnished evidence for why he wasn't back home in his arms. Jacob pleaded with his heartache not to cloud his mind as he examined the garment closely, and then eyed his eldest son with a forlorn look full of disappointment and regret.

"How kind of the wolf to eat my son without even ripping his shirt. I guess even wild animals have some mercy in their hearts," Jacob commented, compressing the grief that was tearing him up inside.

Their faces paled with embarrassment and humiliation as they scanned each other for answers. How did they not think of that? They slipped. They all slipped and at this moment, there was no valid explanation for Jacob's shrewd remark. They underestimated their father, and now they were trapped with their ruthless crime, feeling naked and exposed.

41

"Joseph must have taken his shirt off when we left," Asher stuttered while wiping his tears.

"Then the wolf must have used the shirt as a napkin to wipe his mouth after it was done with its meal," Jacob said with a mix of conviction and sarcasm.

"Didn't I tell you he will doubt us when we tell him the truth?" Reuben asked the rest of them in an offended tone. "No matter what we say, father, you will never believe us. Too bad Joseph is dead! He's the only one who could have defended us because he's the only one you'd listen to."

The word "dead" tugged at Jacob's heart as if it was being ripped out of his chest. His son wasn't dead. He believed deep in his soul that Joseph was alive and well somewhere, and that his amazing vision was yet to come true. This was obviously a horrible trap like he had predicted before. Jacob took a deep breath as he weighed his options on what to do next. Hurl outside and turn every stone looking for Joseph? Or confront his sons with their blatant lie and yell and scream at them until they admit the truth? Or submit to the rage he felt and shatter everything in sight to prevent himself from going insane with this crushingly devastating grief?

No. That would just aggravate them more and feed their jealousy. Any extreme feeling he acted upon now would only put his son's life in danger. It's never a good idea to provoke those who refuse to admit their mistakes while their lies are still searing hot. Even though they were his sons, and he trusted they wouldn't go as far as to kill Joseph, Jacob still didn't trust the devils inside of them...

"If only there were other witnesses in the desert to

confirm our story," Levi took advantage of his father's silence to make him feel bad that he was accusing them of lying. "How sad is it though? You'd probably believe strangers more than you would believe your own sons!"

Benjamin hid behind Leya, shaking uncontrollably, too scared and overwhelmed to utter a word. His stepmother stood frozen with her hand covering her mouth in horror, staring back at her husband and waiting for his response, torn between feeling sorry for her sons and feeling devastated over losing little Joseph.

"My best option now is to stay quiet and ask the Merciful Lord for patience," Jacob announced his final decision. "It's been a long day. I'm sure you would all like to get some rest in your comfortable beds. Have yourselves a good night."

Their father walked away with tears in his eyes. He walked away from the hidden truth, the obvious lies and the shameless guilt that dripped from their mouths. He gave his sons the benefit of the doubt when he let them take Joseph, and now his only salvation was to embrace the certainty that his beloved son was still alive. Jacob was a true believer, and with his faith he knew he would manage to patch up the void in his aching heart. The old man retreated back into the privacy of his room, lifted up his hands to the sky and prayed for the strength to endure this throbbing pain. He prayed for Joseph to stay strong and patient, wherever he was, and hoped his sons would repent and let go of the jealousy and hatred that ate them up inside. He prayed for the wolves inside them to be tamed, and that one day, peace and serenity would bring the whole family back together.

Jacob's prayers rose up to the blessed skies as Benjamin listened from his room, with tears running down his sad, innocent face. The little boy cuddled himself alone in Joseph's bed, shaking and weeping softly, confused about what had happened. Was his brother really dead? Was he really never going to see him again?

Benjamin closed his eyes, wishing this whole nightmare away. Tomorrow, everything will be back to normal, and his brother Joseph will be there helping him make breakfast and twirling him around happily like he did every morning. He refused to think of any other option, for he didn't know how to exist in a world without his loving brother Joseph, the only smile in his life...

***

Alone in the pitch dark hollowness of the well, listening to the hissing echoes of venomous snakes and creeping sounds of deadly scorpions, the little half-naked boy found a dry ledge where he sat hugging his knees, shivering uncontrollably. Joseph thought of his father, and how he must have reacted when he never made it home on time. Jacob was an old man; Joseph feared the shock might affect his health or cause damage to his heart. He thought about little Benjamin, and wondered who made him dinner that night. He liked his food decorated in a certain way and his milk nice and warm, not too hot and not too cold. He must be sad and scared, and no one knew how to soothe him like Joseph did. The echo of wolves howling outside invaded his thoughts, sending a shiver down his spine, as little Joseph buried his face in his knees, trying to block out this crippling fear that was crushing him slowly. He then lifted his head up to the sky and let out a painful cry that shook the walls around him, a scream that spoke of betrayal, deceit and raw agony that he could no longer contain.

"Whatever happens, I know you'll handle it well and stay strong. You're my son, Joseph, and I know I taught you well."

His father's last words suddenly rang in his ears like a wake-up call from a morbid dream. He promised his father he'd make him proud. Joseph blamed his brothers for breaking their promise, and now he was doing the same by submitting to his terror.

"My Lord!" he whispered into the still night, "Give me strength and patience to endure Your will and my destiny, for You are the Most Merciful and the Greatest of all."

As a soft loving mother sways her newborn baby, Joseph's prayers bandaged his heart and soul with a silky warm blanket of holy tenderness. He finally rested his head on the stone ledge and fell asleep with tears rolling down his cheeks and a faint smile.

**

"Jacob?" Leya knocked softly on the closed door after everyone went to sleep. "I know you'd rather be alone for a while. I just came to see how you're holding up, dear."

"Patience is the most fitting at dire times like this, Leya," Jacob said, almost choking on his suppressed tears.

"I can't even begin to describe how sorry I am for your loss. I know how much you loved little Joseph."

"Leya, please! I'm not accepting anyone's condolences. My son is still alive! I know it in my heart, and my heart doesn't lie to me."

"But you've heard Reuben's story and the rest of them," Leya sounded confused. "They were sobbing with so much sadness."

"You were there when I warned them about wolves before they took Joseph away. You heard how insulted Reuben was when I expressed my fear, and they all promised nothing of the sort could ever happen! Yes, they did come back crying, but if tears were evidence of the truth, justice would have no place to live in this world. Never let your sympathy or compassion blind you from seeing the truth."

***

The next day, Joseph woke up disoriented and confused. He couldn't tell if it was still nighttime or the start of a new day. He was hungry, tired, his muscles stiff, and his wounds sore and aching. A little part of him still hoped his brothers would come back and take him home, but when reality struck, it took that yearning away with it. This was his home now; that is, if he managed to survive for a couple more days with no food amidst all these poisonous creatures. Destiny clawed onto his youth with vicious, sharp nails as he imagined what he would have wanted to do as a grown-up. In the darkness he lived in, little Joseph sought patience with dreams and aspirations of a bright future. Prayers, patience and pleasing thoughts are the only keys to survival when you helplessly stare back at the scornful jaws of death.

He chanted a song for his brothers, like a shadowy will of a ghost about to diminish. He poured out his heart into the well of his life, the lyrics prancing above him, witnessing the sad tunes of his oppression and innocence.

Remember me...
When you gather together, remember my loneliness...
When you joke and laugh, remember my silent tears...
Remember me...
When you eat your warm meals, remember my hunger...
And when you sleep in your cosy beds, remember my pain...
Remember me...
When you see a stranger walk by, remember that I'm estranged...
And when you embrace a friend, remember your own flesh and blood...
Remember your little brother...
Remember me...

***

At the break of dawn, Leya, unable to sleep all night, sought comfort in cooking for her family. Holding a pot of hot porridge, she stood motionless by the dining table, staring at Joseph's seat with tears of despair flowing down her face. Her husband was right; her sons' sobbing deceived her last night, and denial got the worst of her judgement. Leya knew her sons were jealous of Joseph, and that maybe they thought him being away would put out the flames of envy burning in their hearts. But standing alone here now, she couldn't help but realise that Joseph was actually the soft smooth clay that held the family together. If her sons did actually take him away, then they'd only extinguished a fire to start a new one, a burning fire of bitter dejection that will be even harder to put out.

The second day went by even slower than the first one, but Joseph tried his best to maintain his patience and strength. Even if his fate was to die in this forsaken well alone, he vowed to face it with courage and pride. Disasters make or break a man, and this experience was just the first test of his willpower, and furthermore, the first real test of his faith. Hunger and pain deserted him while he filled his soul with hope and positivity. As he held on to the dry ledge, Joseph held on to the beautiful memories in his head to be able to get through another night. The innocent smile of Benjamin, the warm embrace of his loving father, and the cheerfully loud dinner times with the fresh food and old family traditions, the thoughts of which lulled him peacefully to sleep. For some reason, he believed in his heart that his fate would take him out of this dark pit to a new blessed light. One day, not far from now, he would unite with his family again, and the nightmare he lived in that night would soon be just a faded memory.

"One day…" he whispered, before closing his eyes and falling asleep.

The following morning, it dawned on Jacob that perhaps this was an examination of his faith, too. It was such a hard test for a father who couldn't stand being away from his beloved son for even one hour. As much as he tried to stay strong, his heart was still bleeding inside. He went to Joseph's room every night to get a whiff of his clothes, and then broke down crying until the sun came up again with no reassuring news of his whereabouts. Jacob couldn't help but feel suffocated and disappointed in his sons, who still stood their ground about their forged story. It was impossible to look them in the eye without seeing Joseph's image huddled alone in a corner, scared and confused. Jacob took a deep breath as he stepped outside to the backyard to check on the animals, just as his dearest son used to do. He noticed someone was there already; his youngest boy, who was so engrossed in a one-way conversation, he didn't even hear his father walk in.

"Do you believe in heaven, Mr. Muscles?" Jacob heard Benjamin whisper to the beautiful horse in the barn. "Do you think my brother left me and went to heaven?"

He brushed its hair softly with his fingers, as tears streamed down his cheeks. "How can he leave me alone? Doesn't he know he's all I have in this world? What will I do without him now?"

The little boy fell to his knees and sobbed sadly for a long time. His father Jacob watched from behind the wall, each tear like corroding acid burning a hole in his heart. The family was falling apart slowly, and as much as he wanted to soothe little Benjamin, he didn't know how to explain why his big brothers took his beloved Joseph away. Jacob pulled himself together. He had to learn how to survive without Joseph, the light of his life, and still find it within him to forgive his sons, who had torn him away from his heart.

"Benjamin?" Jacob walked up to him slowly.

"Yes, father?" The little boy wiped his tears with the back of his hands.

"Come here, son." Jacob sat on the ground and held his little child in his arms. "I know you're sad, and I know you probably have a million unanswered questions in your head. I just need you to have faith in the Lord and stay strong for me, please."

"Where is Joseph, father? Where is he?" Benjamin cried again.

"I don't know where he is, but I know in my heart he's fine and that one day we will see him again."

"How can you be so sure?" Benjamin pouted.

"It's because I have faith that the best is yet to come. You can't have a rainbow without rain, right? And good things come to those who wait patiently, Ben."

"I've been waiting and waiting for him to come back but he still hasn't come! If this is the rain, then where is the rainbow, father?"

Jacob kissed his son's forehead and softly played with his hair as he explained lovingly, "Did I ever tell you the story of your great grandparents before?"

"About grandfather Isaac and grandfather Abraham?" Benjamin exclaimed.

"Yes. Now grandfather Abraham was married to a lovely Egyptian woman named Hajar, and together they had baby Ishmael, your great uncle."

"Is that grandfather Isaac's half-brother?" Benjamin wondered out loud.

"That's right, son!" Jacob smiled as he positioned himself to sit more comfortably. "A long time ago, his wife Hajar and their baby son, Ishmael, found themselves alone in a deserted land, with hardly any food or water. It was a dry, isolated valley between two mountains, with no trees or fruits or wells or anything at all. She was all alone with a crying, thirsty baby and there was no one around to ask for help."

"What did she do?" The little boy's eyes widened double their size.

"When baby Ishmael wouldn't stop crying, Hajar rested him carefully on the ground and ran to the top of the nearest mountain, hoping she'd get a better view of the valley, to see if there were any people there."

"Did she find anyone?" Benjamin asked hopefully.

"No, she didn't, so she hurried down and ran to the other mountain and climbed it to the very top. Hajar scanned the whole area from above, hoping maybe she'd find a faraway well or fruit tree."

"Did she find anything this time?" Benjamin asked again.

"No, she didn't."

"So what did she do? She already climbed both mountains and couldn't see anything!"

"She went back again quickly to the first mountain, climbed it all the way up, and searched again, hoping maybe this time she would find something new," Jacob replied.

"She didn't give up?" Benjamin asked, slowly understanding what his father was teaching him.

"No, Benjamin. She didn't give up. In fact, she kept running back and forth under the hot burning sun seven times in a row, believing in her heart that the Lord would send help, and saying over and over 'My Lord is the Most Merciful of all'. This is when the most amazing thing happened!"

"What happened?" the little boy wondered curiously.

"Hajar went back to the spot where she had left her baby son crying, and there, out of nowhere, a spring of pure holy water erupted suddenly from the ground!"

"Wow! In the middle of the dry desert?" Benjamin marvelled.

"Yes! It was a miracle from the Great Lord. He rewarded Hajar's patience and determination with a stream of blessed water called 'Zamzam' that would last till eternity and beyond."

"But why didn't the Lord give the water in the beginning when the baby first started crying?"

"Because life is nothing but a test, Benjamin. Hajar didn't cry and give up. She knew in her heart that the Lord would take care of her and the baby. Imagine her happiness after running back and forth, thirsty and tired, and then finally finding that stream."

"It must have been a fantastic feeling!" Benjamin smiled.

"Yes, it was fantastic I'm sure," Jacob laughed.

"Just like it will be when we meet Joseph again!"

"'Fantastic' won't even begin to describe the happiness I'll feel when that day comes, son," Jacob said, his mind drifting far away.

"I miss Joseph so much, father."

"I miss him too, Benjamin. But you know, just because you can't see a person doesn't mean he's not there. Joseph is alive in my heart. It's a little trick I taught myself to stay strong and patient. Do you want to try it, too?"

"Yes, but how?"

"Feel your brother, Ben. Think of what he loves and take care of it, and remember what he dislikes and stay away from it. Do the things he always taught you to do and keep his memory blooming until he's back. Do you think you can do that, son?"

"He loved saying prayers at sunrise and listening to your stories about our ancestors, and loved helping everyone out," Benjamin replied. "He liked everything clean and organised and made sure everyone was comfortable and happy, even the animals."

"There you go! What else?"

"He loved to learn and discover new things!" Benjamin's eyes sparkled, "And didn't really like it when I was mad at my brothers. It made him very sad," he added, lowering his head miserably.

"Are you mad at your brothers, son?" Jacob asked carefully.

"I was, but I don't want to be mad at them anymore. I don't want to make Joseph sad."

"That's my boy." Jacob hugged him lovingly.

"You know what else Joseph loved?"

"What else?"

"He loved to see you smile, father."

"I'm smiling, Benjamin…" Jacob smiled sadly, "I'm smiling because I know Joseph will come back one day, and he will make us all proud…"

***

Instead of spending his time in the bleak shaft waiting for his destiny, Joseph decided to seize every minute the best way he knew how to, given the circumstances. Between prayers and chanting songs to soothe his loneliness, Joseph taught himself how to meditate and understand his inner self. It was a powerful energy that gave a person intense power and wisdom. He focused on his father's voice, mentally replaying his wise teachings. His thoughts and contemplations made intricate designs in his head, and mysteries were resolved before him like rays of light. He envisioned stories his father Jacob had told him about his ancestors who had struggled in their lives before. His great grandfather's story was full of hardships and valuable lessons that left listeners truly mesmerised. Abraham was a true icon of faith and patience, and Joseph had his blood running through his veins. It was his duty to keep his grandfather's legend alive.

Many incredible events in this world seem like misfortunes at first but are in fact blessings in disguise. Life is filled with trials and hardships, for that is how true believers and weak, faithless hearts are revealed. There must be a race filled with obstacles for people to come out winners, to truly appreciate their rewards. Joseph believed in his heart that no matter what crops up, the Lord will always do what is best for His creation, and if miracles happened before, they can always happen again, for our history is what defines our future. Fear and sadness were feelings a person could control if he or she really wanted to, and instead of submitting to them, Joseph chose to submit to the One and Only Lord above.

"My Lord!" he repeated over and over again. "Give me strength and patience to endure Your will and my destiny, for You are the Most Merciful and the Greatest of all."

Joseph couldn't tell how many days it had been now since the time he was brutally cast off in the well by his brothers, and yet instead of giving up, he expected the best from the Lord and stayed optimistic. While he was absorbed in his sincere prayers, the little boy suddenly heard a sound, then felt a strange object lightly bump against his head. He gasped and rubbed his eyes, trying to regain focus. The immense darkness of the pit made it difficult to recognise anything anymore. Joseph reached out to touch the object dangling above his head and pulled it down with all his might. It was a big bucket tied to a rope all the way up from over the well. He heard echoes and sounds of men yelling outside, and felt a rush through his whole body. After days and nights of agonizing silence, interrupted only by howls of wolves and caws of crows, some people had finally found their way to this deserted spot! Joseph burst into both laughter and happy tears, amazed at how his positivity had resulted in a positive outcome when there appeared to be no chance of survival. He called out for help in a frail voice then held onto the rope with all the power he could muster as he felt his whole body being lifted up slowly.

Joseph knew his father would send someone to look for him, and that maybe his brothers would come back to their senses after giving their feelings of guilt some time to sink in. Soon, Joseph would be taken back home to submerge himself in his father's warm, loving embrace. As he was being drawn up slowly away from the darkness into the light, the little boy thanked the Lord for His blessings, feeling more certain than ever that miracles do happen.

Squinting with eyes half-open, Joseph came face to face with a big greasy man. He had a visible brown scar across his left cheek, and his bald head reflected the rays of the hot sun as harshly as the pale sand did. The stranger smiled wickedly at Joseph, showing countless missing teeth.

"Look what we got here," the man slurred. "Young, fresh meat. And it's not even my birthday yet!"

Chapter Four

Earlier that day, a group of caravan merchants travelling from Syria went deeper into the desert looking for water to quench their thirst. They were running out, and the well they glanced from afar was their only prospect for survival. The men tied up their camels nearby and waited for their water-fetchers to run and check it out.

"I swear if this is another dry well, I'm going to beat one of you up," the big bully merchant threatened the rest. "It's too long of a journey to go out of our way just because you wimps can't take the heat!"

"It's been a whole day and we haven't had a sip of water. And we still have a lot of ground to cover, man!" another cranky seller complained.

"You watch your tone with me, you idiot! I already need an excuse to take my anger out on someone after the stunt you all pulled last week."

"It wasn't our fault the deal never went through. You wanted to pull the wool over the buyer's eyes, except he was smart enough to double check the goods before paying for them."

"Are you calling me a swindler, you miserable fool? I'll make sure I double check your worthless corpse before I throw it to the dogs!" the bully snapped, ready to attack.

"Look! He is waving for us to go there," a skinny merchant spoke frantically to shift the angry man's focus. "He must have found lots of water and needs help carrying the buckets!"

The merchants went to help out with the water-drawing, cursing and grumbling about the hot weather and the worthless stock they carried across countries for almost no money. It had been a dismal season for the grim traders, and if their luck wasn't going to smile at them soon, someone would have to pay the price.

Inside the well, Joseph's heart was pounding with thrill and anticipation when he grabbed onto the bucket that appeared to revive his hope. It had been three whole days that he'd been trapped inside there alone. He could hear voices of strangers yelling outside and tugging at the rope attached to the water bucket. And it seemed like more men had joined to help pull him out. "Thanks to the Lord!" he repeated all the way up, out of the darkness into the light. All the misery and pain he felt were easily swept away by the immense joy of that moment. As he approached the top of the well, he squinted his eyes to adjust them to the sunlight, trying to recognise the features and voices of the people rescuing him.

"Look what we got here," the greasy boy with the visible scar and missing teeth smiled back at Joseph.

"Is this a real human being, or did I get a sunstroke and I'm finally seeing angels before dropping dead?" the skinny man marvelled at the beautiful young boy.

"Looks like our luck has changed after all!" the big bully man said. "I see money signs flashing before me. You guys get my drift, right?" He winked.

The merchants were scrutinising him as if he were a porcelain doll for sale. Joseph could hardly even stand up, let alone have the energy to walk, when they urged him to move to where they had camped earlier. He was hungry, tired, and barely able to focus anymore or even understand what they were saying. Hopefully these people knew their way around the city and would have no trouble taking him home.

"Thank you for helping me," Joseph said politely. "I'm truly grateful for your kindness."

"Not just pretty, he's well-bred too!" one of the merchants laughed mockingly. "You think we can charge extra for that?" he asked the rest, after spitting out a shot of phlegm on the ground.

"I'm sure my father will have a handsome reward for

you; he's a very generous man," Joseph said, trying to interpret their conversation in a positive light.

"Shut your mouth, pretty boy!" the man barked spitefully. "Slaves don't speak without permission."

"Slaves?" Joseph asked in a horrified tone.

"Wait! He has a family! What if someone recognises him and gets us in trouble?" the skinny man panicked when they reached the camped caravan.

With no further ado, the bully grabbed an empty smelly straw bag from their luggage and stuffed little Joseph inside of it. "There! Problem solved," he laughed, his big belly shaking up and down with amusement.

"You're a genius!" the skinny merchant exclaimed, hoping the bully would remember that compliment the next time he lost his temper.

"No, please, let me out!" Joseph struggled weakly inside the sack. "Take me home, please. My father will pay you, I promise!"

"You don't have a father no more. From this day on you will have a master, someone who can make use of that pretty face of yours," the bully laughed hysterically before shoving Joseph hard to shut him up. "It's a long way to Egypt, you little whiner! So you better behave yourself on the road or you'll have to face my wrath. And I promise you, there's nothing pretty about that!"

What happened to the people in this world? What was wrong with adults that they abused children this way? Weren't they supposed to guide them when they were lost and soothe them when they were hurt?

In a world where ethics had little meaning and injustice prevailed, the young boy was too weak and drained to struggle. He pleaded for their mercy as they laughed

and mounted their camels quickly. Just when he thought he'd been salvaged into the light, Joseph was back to the dreaded darkness again, with more sadness and pain, and even further away from home.

The Egyptian marketplace, or the Souq, was as busy as a beehive at this time of year. Quaysides of the Nile River were crammed with buyers and merchants from different countries dealing in all kinds of trade. Farmers came with their eager, shrill wives to sell fresh fruits, vegetables and grains. Sailors and travellers roamed the market looking for opportunities to benefit from, before heading back home to their families. Small-scale merchants sat in stalls displaying all sorts of goods and stocks, from handmade jewellery and perfumes, to bread, fish and meat. The place burst with vitality and live auctions for the highest bidders on fine breeds of cattle and human outcasts turned to slaves. In a highly polarised society, the Souq was one of the rare places where the elite mingled with peasants and hard-working labourers, for there was always the prospect of a profitable trade.

Joseph surveyed the dynamic scene with astonishment, now that he was finally free from the prickly straw sack and chained with handcuffs, ready to be advertised amidst a crowd of vultures. It seemed he'd been travelling for many long weeks, as he finally gave up on debating and persuading the men to let him go. They didn't waste time in getting rid of him out of fear of being found out, so they sold him to the first buyer for a meagre price; only a few dirhams and not even a second glance. From there on, Joseph was sold from one slave market to the next, patiently enduring the swaggering and mockery of the more seasoned slaves he had to share space with while waiting for the next highest bidder. Finally arriving at one of the most elite slave markets in the city, Joseph stood tall and proud, facing the destiny that kept catching up with him since the day he had been separated from his family. The merchants who had picked him up surrounded him like crows, impatient to seal a good deal on their innocent prey.

"Ladies and gentlemen, feast your eyes on the beauty that stands before you!" the short fat merchant bellowed to the people gathering around them. "The prettiest slave in history is on the market for sale. Feast your eyes! Young meat, ladies and gentlemen. Who can put a price on such grace?"

The son of the noble Jacob, grandson of the noble Abraham, and the descendant of the most honoured and dignified ancestors, stood in chains at the slave market waiting to be sold like cheap merchandise. Joseph stared back at the foreign faces and the piercing eyes, wondering who would be his new owner. His attention then shifted to his surroundings that were so different from the small city he came from. He could see the huge temples and gigantic stone structures across the horizon, engraved with their special hieroglyphic symbols. Rolling desert land lay west of the Nile Valley, and mountains rose to the east. Many of the visible houses seemed to belong to the typical middle-class society; mostly narrow two-storey buildings built with bricks of dried mud, and trunks of palm trees supporting their flat roofs. The Egyptian people resembled his own people in a way; dark-skinned and dark-haired farmers dressed in white linen came to the market barefoot, with their almost naked children tagging along, too hot to wear clothes in the scorching hot weather. Merchants spread wet mats on the ground to help cool them off, while most women wore wigs to protect their heads from the blazing heat of the sun. It seemed the number of people drawn to inspect Joseph was getting larger by the minute. The calls for bids woke him up from his momentary daze, and as he looked ahead of him, he noticed a huge chariot hauled by two beautiful black Arabian horses making its way through the narrow roads.

The yelling and bargaining suddenly faded to amused whispers when an affluent-looking man in the finest attire stepped out and made his way to the front, followed by two mean sturdy guards. He took one look at the young slave on sale, snapped his fingers at the slave trader who came running, and then with just a nod and a quick exchange of money, he took Joseph home.

People called him the Potiphar, or "The Aziz" in Arabic, which translated to "The Majestic", and indeed he was. The Aziz was one of the most prosperous lords in the country, and Egypt's leading Chief Minister of Finance. Men and women bowed with respect just hearing the approaching sound of his footsteps. He lived in a huge mansion, furnished with lavish interiors and waited upon by tens of servants and guards. The Aziz had the wealth, the power, the status, and the beautiful wife, but was never granted any children. The moment he saw little Joseph at the market, his heart instantly warmed to him as he yearned for a son with his beautiful looks and courteous demeanour.

"Take these handcuffs and chains off!" the Aziz ordered his guards before dismissing them. "What's your name, son?" he then asked Joseph in a gentle tone.

"My name is Joseph, your Highness."

"Where do you come from?"

"From a city called Canaan in Palestine."

"How did you end up here? Where's your family?"

"We simply follow the tracks of our destiny, your Highness."

"You seem very wise for one so young."

"Thanks to my father. He has been blessed with prudence and knowledge." Joseph paused for a sad moment then added, "He is a very wise man."

Even though his hair was dishevelled and his robe ragged and old, the young boy still glowed with an ethereal light, like a handsome prince trapped in a different time and place. He stood barefoot on the expensively decorated palace floor, his body bruised and aching, and his head pounding with pain. He couldn't decide what he felt at this moment, for the events in his life were crashing so hard against the tides of time, that nothing made sense anymore. Not so long ago, he was kissing his loving father goodnight before telling Benjamin a bedtime story. Today, he was in a foreign country, abducted and enslaved.

The Aziz stared at Joseph for a long time and then said, "You will not be treated as a slave in my house. You will be free to move around and have your private space to sleep and rest. You won't be ill-treated if you behave yourself. Do not betray my trust in you, Joseph."

"I give you my word, your Highness. I appreciate

your kindness and I will stay faithful and loyal to you for as long as I stay here."

The Aziz went to see his wife after ordering the housekeepers to show Joseph to his room. She was sitting in her luxurious bedroom suite, gazing out of the window at her beautiful acres of lush gardens.

"I heard we got a new delivery from the slave market," his wife, Zulaikha, commented absentmindedly as her husband walked in.

"No, not a new slave," the Aziz replied quickly, sounding offended. "He's a beautiful young boy who was separated from his family. He seems to have a decent background. I'm sure we can benefit from his stay with us, or perhaps adopt him as a son."

"You want us to adopt a slave?! Don't you think that's a little too desperate?"

Zulaikha was a beautiful woman in her early twenties. She got married to the Aziz at a very young age in an extravagant wedding, which people talked about for months and months to follow. Almost every young female in the city envied her for the life she gained in the royal palace, where she was treated like a celebrated queen. Her husband loved her deeply, and appreciated her for never complaining they couldn't have any children. Even though he gave her everything else she wanted before she even asked, the Aziz still felt his beautiful wife wasn't happy. She had that distant look in her eyes sometimes, as if there was something missing. It was one of the reasons why he brought Joseph home, for perhaps that's what his wife needed to fill the void in her life: a young son she could love and take care of.

"There's something special about this boy… I can't explain it," the Aziz said in a warm tone.

"You are the 'Aziz'! What would people say if you took an outcast for a son?!"

"I have all this wealth, knowledge and power and no one to inherit it after I pass away. It breaks my heart every time I think of it."

"Don't worry, dear. Your wealth will always be in good hands," his wife smiled to herself.

"Besides, it's not completely unheard of. I mean, affluent men adopt skilled boys with prospects for a bright future. I thought that's the one thing you longed for, Zulaikha. I know deep down inside it saddens you too that we can't have children."

"We promised ourselves we would not discuss this subject anymore!" Zulaikha got up, refusing to admit her inner feelings. "I told you a million times before, I gave up on the idea of a family a long time ago. I don't want you to buy me a son, thank you very much!"

"You can make him your personal attendant if you like. I know he's a young boy, but he has the mentality and disposition of a grown man. Just make sure he's comfortable and treated well. Do not treat him like you usually treat the other slaves. That's all I'm asking."

"Very well, dear," Zulaikha calmed her husband down with her soft tone. "Consider it done. I'll take care of him and make him feel at home."

"I have a feeling you'll really like him, Zulaikha," the Aziz added before setting out. "You'll know what I mean when you see him. He's probably the most beautiful human being you will ever lay eyes on in your entire life."

Zulaikha glanced at her reflection in the mirror and fixed her hair, the fake smile disappearing the moment her husband closed the door behind him. "The most beautiful human being? What a thoughtful thing to say to your wife," she mumbled sarcastically. "Well, let's see if you're right. I've been looking for a project to keep me busy, and ogling a handsome stranger while spending your money is just as good as any, my dear..."

Chaptër Fïvë

Benjamin gazed at the bright full moon and saw his brother's beautiful face shine through it. He knew if Joseph was indeed still alive, he would be staring at the moon at the exact same time he was. Maybe it was an illusion or a crazy fantasy, but it remained the only notion keeping Benjamin going: the hope of his brother returning home one day.

"Wish you were here," Benjamin whispered his only wish on his birthday before closing his eyes. "Goodnight, Joseph. Sweet dreams…"

In the privacy of his spacious room, Joseph thanked the Lord for all His blessings. After weeks of darkness, deprivation and hunger, he finally had warm meals, hot showers and a comfortable bed. He was given clean sets of clothes and grooming supplies which were fit enough for the children of royalty. His job was fairly simple: follow the rich woman everywhere she went and attend to her needs. He was obedient, well-mannered, and with his charming looks and pleasantly cheerful attitude, he won the love and respect of everyone around him, especially Zulaikha, who instantly warmed to Joseph from the very first time she saw him.

Days, months and years went by, and Joseph grew

into an extraordinary man adorned with exceptional beauty and captivating perfection. He took on more responsibilities as he grew older, conquering every single opportunity to educate himself and absorb the teachings of his master, the Aziz, who tutored and trained him with passion and enthusiasm. He learnt all about the Egyptian economy and foreign trade affairs, and watched closely how as Chief Minister, he handled any deficits or discrepancies in the system with expertise. Joseph soon became his right-hand man. He was smart, eloquent and graceful; he mastered the art of effective influence and inspirational speech, making his character even more irresistible. The Aziz appreciated his honesty, loyalty and eagerness to learn, which made him put Joseph in charge of his household, and honour him as a noble son of his own.

However, despite all this freedom and luxury, Joseph's heart still ached with longing for his father and little brother. In moments of solitude, his thoughts travelled to his home in Palestine, yearning for even a glimpse of their smiles. Not a day passed him by without shedding a tear of buried sadness, or without sending out prayers filled with warmth and devotion to his loved ones back home. His older brothers denied him of the simplest pleasures in life, greeting his father every morning and tucking his baby brother in bed every night. Of course, he wasn't a baby anymore now, was he?

Joseph drowned in his memories with a sad smile, then quickly adjusted back to his current life and focused on his numerous tasks. He wasn't the kind of person to give in to depression or self-pity; even though he was a very sensational young man, he was also a practical, ambitious one. If he couldn't be in the place he loved with the people he cherished most in the world, he would let himself learn to love the place he was in and warm to the new people who were slowly becoming his family.

"I need you to escort me to the temple, Joseph," Zulaikha commanded before stepping out into the front courtyard, clad in a long tight dress with shoulder straps and a dark wig.

"I'd be happy to escort you, my lady," one of the top army officers suggested cordially, delighted to be of service.

"I said Joseph!" Zulaikha snapped rudely, appalled at the man's interference.

"After you, my lady," Joseph said politely, ignoring the jealous looks the officer gave him.

"I also need you to cancel all your errands and tasks for today. I'll be spending the whole day at the temple for the big festival and I need you with me."

"I'm sure I can manage both, my lady," Joseph replied decently, opening the door to her carriage while keeping his eyes averted.

"She's getting overly attached to that Joseph boy, don't you think?" the army officer asked one of his peers in a bitter tone as he watched the royal chariot depart the premises.

"I'd say she is. She hardly goes anywhere without him now," his friend replied in a low voice.

"What does she see in him? He's nothing but a mere slave."

"Shhh! Watch what you say about Joseph. Do you want the Aziz to have our heads?!"

Zulaikha stared at Joseph the whole ride to the temple, wondering what he was thinking as he gazed outside the little window. In the many years he'd lived in the palace, he only let people get close to a certain limit, maintaining an invisible barrier around his heart. He was always very proper and respectable, always alert and attentive, never missing even the finest detail. As much as it confused her at first as to why her husband trusted and cared for him so much, she now slowly began to see why. There was something special about him, something unusual about his speech and even more surreal about his silence. Never did he try to impress or win anyone over with his charm and handsome looks, and yet everything about him was beyond impressive. She couldn't deny she was getting attached to him, but then again, he grew up before her eyes, and she got to witness what an extraordinary young man he had become. Perhaps he was no slave after all. He was more of a friend or even a role model. She really wanted to admit the truth. Whatever the label was, she just knew her heart was filled with joy and peace whenever she was around Joseph. His mere presence gave her a rush, and that's all she needed for now.

People were only allowed to enter the temple courtyard on festival days, and Zulaikha made sure she was the first to visit the gods with her entourage, where the priest allocated a private space and time for her to perform her prayers. Due to her affluence and appeal, she was also sometimes allowed inside the sanctuary, the special place where only high-ranking pastors and kings were permitted in. She asked the rest to wait outside and accompanied Joseph to the mysterious shrine of the gods. He inspected the decorated walls as he walked beside her down the narrow path, well aware now of what each symbol and drawing represented. Zulaikha was enthralled by the enigmatic aura of the place, captured in a state of deep veneration as she prostrated to the still statue shaped in the form of a female with a headdress of horns.

"Prostrate to goddess Hathor, Joseph. She is the wife of Horus. She has the power to bless your life if you worship her from the heart," Zulaikha whispered.

"With all due respect, my lady, I only prostrate to the One and Only Lord, and no one else," Joseph replied politely.

"These are my gods, Joseph," Zulaikha whispered heatedly. "Show some respect!"

"I cannot stop you from worshipping your god, my lady," he answered calmly, "but you can never force me to respect or bow to an idol made of stone."

"This is the goddess of love and joy," Zulaikha marvelled. "She is the 'Mistress of Heaven' and the 'Lady of Stars', the embodiment of love, romance and beauty. She's the mother incarnation of dance, music and sensuality. How can one not worship her?"

"I ask the exact opposite question," Joseph argued. "How can we worship handmade gods and ask them for things they are powerless to provide? Love evolves from within our souls... Not through some stone statue."

"Love evolves from within us?" she repeated softly.

"Yes, my lady. All those beautiful feelings we have are bestowed upon us from the Lord. Love is a seed you

water with mercy and compassion till it blooms like a fruitful tree. It's pure and selfless… Love is loyalty, forgiveness and striving to make others happy."

"You speak as if you come from a different world where everything is perfect and complete. Sometimes you're as clear as the sky, and other times as mysterious as the moonlit night," Zulaikha said as they left the temple together.

"I'm just a normal person, my lady," Joseph replied humbly, "and I believe the answers are there for those who seek the truth."

"There's nothing ordinary about you, Joseph," Zulaikha said softly. "You grew up in our home before our eyes, and I've seen for myself how much of an amazingly unique young man you've turned out to be."

"I'll take that as a compliment, thank you," Joseph smiled. "You and your kind husband have been very good to me, and treated me like a dear son. I really don't know how I'll ever repay you."

"You can repay me by never mentioning the 'son' part ever again," Zulaikha laughed nervously. "In case you haven't noticed, I'm too young to be your mother."

Why was she so offended when he compared them to his parents? Zulaikha scolded herself silently on the way back to the palace. True, her husband did raise him like offspring of his own, but that didn't indicate anything about her taking the place of his mother. Yes, she did care for him all these years, except soon she was starting to realise that her fondness of him wasn't the motherly kind but something very different. He brought out a new side of her; an inner affection that only brimmed to the surface when he was around. His smile took her to a different world, and being alone with him was more exciting and feverish than anything else she'd ever known in her life. Slowly, Joseph was becoming the reason she felt alive inside. As she bid him goodnight with a yearning gaze and went up to her bedroom suite, Zulaikha wondered what that ardent feeling was called. She lit up the candles around her dresser and stared back at herself in the mirror for a long, silent moment.

"Wake up, Zulaikha!" she whispered to herself in the still night. "You are the mighty Aziz's wife, and Joseph is the young boy he bought at the slave market!"

The lonely, beautiful woman lay down on her lavish bed and closed her eyes, trying to regain the scattered thoughts that were being repeatedly overpowered by Joseph's gorgeous smile and captivating eyes. Her feelings were becoming undeniable at this point. Zulaikha put a hand to her pounding heart and sighed softly.

"I think I'm falling in love with you, Joseph…"

Chapter Six

She stood on the terrace in the small hours of the morning, watching him water the flowers in her garden with devoted attention. Zulaikha, the Aziz's wife, found herself searching for Joseph when he wasn't around, and missing him when he was away. She couldn't help but stare at his beauty; he was exquisitely handsome in a way that was beyond surreal. His eyes were like the deep sea; expressive, dreamy and magnetising. His face was as luminous as the full moon, glowing with a magic shimmer, even in the brightness of daylight. His hair was dark and soft like falls of gleaming silk, and his figure strong and muscular like a great warrior in a battlefield. Just stepping into his mid-twenties, he merged youth and maturity together in a cascade of exuberant vigour and heavenly grace. His voice was like music to her ears, and his smile was as hypnotizing as a blissful spell. The prominent chief's wife standing on the high terrace was falling in love with the slave who grew up in her home, and to her disappointment, the more she tried to get closer to him, the more he backed away.

"A lady with your power, wealth and intelligence can make a difference in this world," Joseph once told her while she stared back at him, mesmerised by his charm

and charisma. "Perhaps you can use some of your free time to help those in need."

"Don't you have needs, Joseph?" she smiled suggestively.

"My Lord blessed me in so many ways, and left me needing nothing but His Grace and Forgiveness. My aim is to give a helping hand to the less fortunate, and with all due respect, I highly suggest you do the same. Now if you will excuse me, my lady, I need to get back to work."

His firmness in the face of her seduction only heightened the passion she had for the enchanting young man. He was obviously implying she was courting him out of sheer boredom and a need for a new challenge. He repeatedly yet artfully advised her to abstain from sinful thoughts and find herself a useful activity. He almost convinced her to give money to charity for heaven's sake! Joseph had a great passion and love for the poor; it drove her crazy seeing those peasant girls and worthless servants seek his help and advice.

Jealousy haunted her even in her sleep, just thinking about him being amiable and respectfully pleasant to other women. She was the high and mighty Zulaikha! The woman who controlled hundreds of men with the click of her fingers. A mere attendant like him made her weak in the knees and that made her extremely frustrated, and even more stubborn and persistent. All she wanted was to spend more time with him. She needed Joseph to notice her and reciprocate the love she had for him.

Looking at her beautiful reflection in the golden-framed mirror, Zulaikha drowned in her own shameless fantasies. Joseph was right. She did need something to occupy her time with. Now she had finally found a challenging venture and a beautiful one indeed.

What about your husband? the voice in her head would ask occasionally.

The chaste side of Zulaikha looked the other way. The truth was her husband was too busy worrying about his empire to notice his wife's feelings for the son they never had. He trusted Joseph completely for he was the most honourable man he'd ever met. At the same time, the Aziz gave Zulaikha hardly any attention. He chose to live in denial that the connection between him and his beautiful lonely wife was lost and instead made up for it by giving her the most expensive gifts money could buy. It didn't occur to the powerful man that his wife had other desires, and they didn't include rare gems or imported perfume.

As months went by, Zulaikha's womanly coy was constantly yet gently turned down time after time. Joseph was now avoiding even being in the same place as her. He always made excuses about being busy with work, and made sure one of the servants or guards were present nearby when the Aziz's wife requested his attendance. Her subtle tactics to lure him came to no avail. She was running out of patience, until one day she bribed one of her servants to escort him to her bedroom suite on account of an urgent matter. After walking him down the long hall leading to her private suite, Zulaikha motioned the servant to leave from the nearest door and quickly locked it behind her with a special key.

They were finally alone.

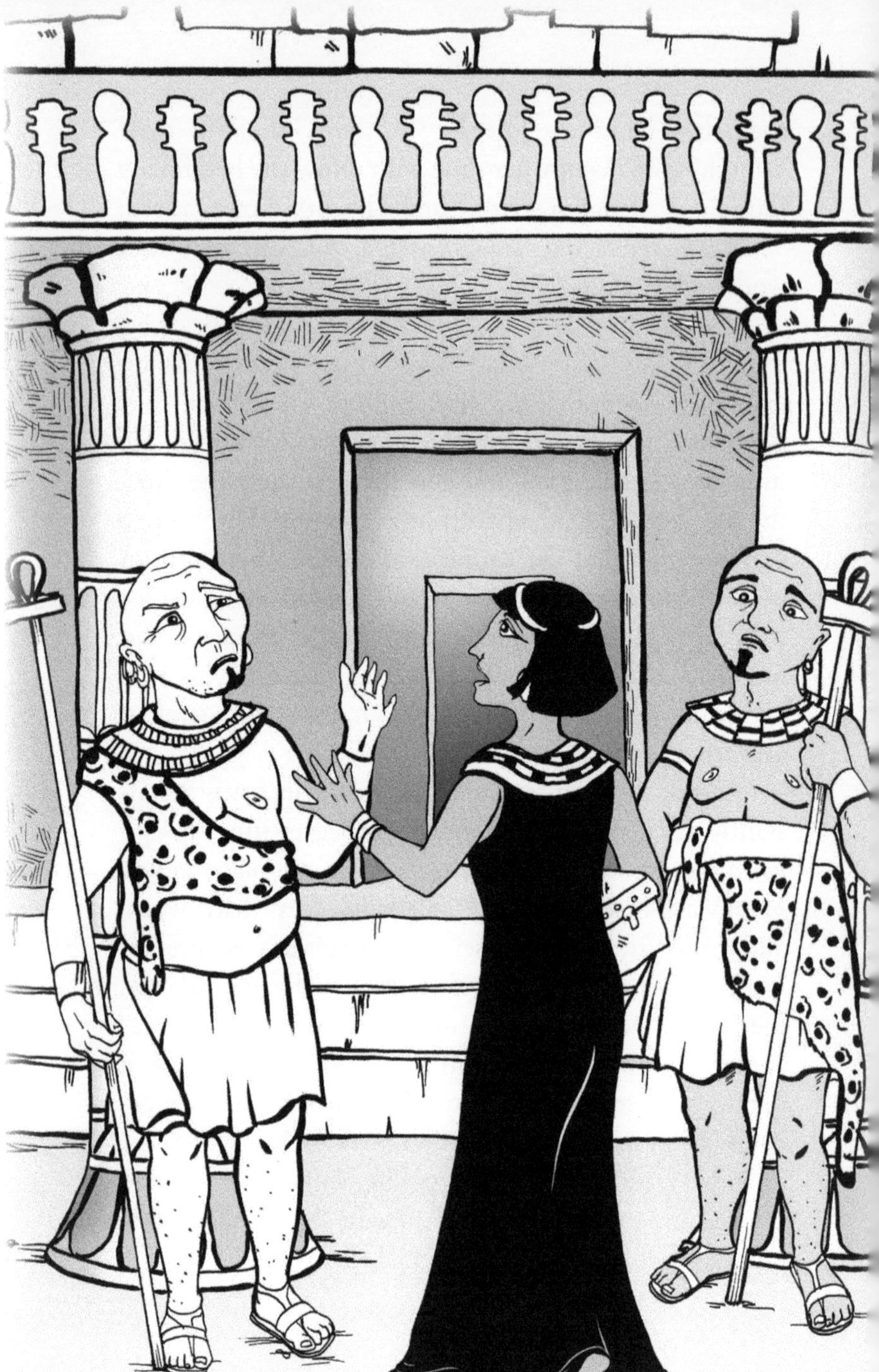

The lavishness of her royal bedroom faded in comparison to Joseph's majestic appeal. He stood tall and proud beneath the intricately designed blue and yellow ceiling. His shadow seemed to glow on the expensive tiled floor as he avoided eye contact with the determined woman. Time seemed to pause in awe of his presence. Zulaikha wondered if it was possible to even attempt to describe his beauty... He had a mystical quality that left people entranced in a splendid haze. She could literally hear her heart pounding every time she glanced at this magnificent young man, and it tore her apart that he didn't feel the same way about her.

"My lady, what can I do for you this evening?" Joseph asked politely, his eyes fixed on the floor.

"Look at me, Joseph," she said in a soft, pleading voice.

"One of the servants said you needed me for an urgent matter that could not wait. I'd appreciate if you tell me what it is so I can go back to work," he said with his gaze still lowered.

"All you care about is work, work, work! What about me, Joseph? Don't you care about me?"

"You are my master's wife, and you've both been very generous to me since I came here. If I have done anything to upset or offend you, I do apologise for it, my lady."

"You not noticing my love for you upsets me, Joseph!" she said.

Joseph remained silent. He took one swift look around the suite and noticed all the doors leading to the adjacent rooms were locked with a number of heavy metal latches, not just the main door he came from. He was trapped, and since he was in charge, he figured the timing wasn't a coincidence either. Zulaikha knew her husband wouldn't be home for hours and of course none of the other slaves dared come near her chambers unless specifically called for. She'd obviously been planning for this night, and he had no idea how to stop her without causing a huge scandal.

The beautiful, noble woman was offering herself to him in a locked room away from the world. She reached out to run her fingers through his hair, and as much as he was deprived of tenderness and soft touches, Joseph resisted her wicked advances and took a step back.

"I come close to you, yet you distance yourself from me?" she whispered.

"I desire by that the closeness of my Lord. God sees and hears everything, my lady," he replied.

"You're right. Even though our love is real and intense, but I understand why you're scared. Wait, I have an idea." She grabbed her shawl and threw it to cover the stone idol she cherished on her bedside table. "Forgive me, God. But you can't watch."

"That's not what I meant!" Joseph was extremely offended. "Worrying about a stone statue is.... it's foolishness! I refer to our creator Almighty Allah, the One and Only God."

"Need I remind you that you are my slave? And that it is your job to obey me?"

"Not if it means disobeying my Lord."

"Joseph... I have belittled myself so much trying to possess you. Look at me. I spent the whole day preparing myself for you. You have no other choice but to obey my orders."

"Obedience is different to disloyalty, my lady. Your husband trusts me. He gave me a home and treated me with kindness and respect. I'll never betray him this way. Never!"

"It will be our little secret, my love," she boldly leaned in closer.

"I think this conversation is over. If you will excuse me, please!" He put his hand up to stop her from getting any closer then turned around and hurried away.

"No!" she screamed, running fast to stop him from leaving.

Sin and virtue raced down the hall for the locked door, before Zulaikha grabbed Joseph's shirt with infuriation, with such force that it tore away from his back. Zulaikha allowed herself to submit to her illicit desires, but the rejection she got in return was driving her completely insane, making her lose her dignity and pride along the sinful path of immorality. Joseph struggled to unlock the door to escape her tight grip and relentless begging to remain. He finally freed himself from her enticing trap and opened the door to righteousness with the mighty force of a stallion running for its life.

It was at that same moment that the Aziz was heading out to meet with some friends after a long meeting with his subordinates, yet contrary to his usual routine, he decided to drop by and see his wife first. There, standing behind the unlocked door of secrets, Joseph came face to face with the man who entrusted him with his household and gave him full freedom. The scene at the doorway left little for interpretation. His wife's face flushed blood red while she glanced quickly at Joseph, who stood there dishevelled and exasperatingly silent. Guilt, innocence and

betrayal pierced through the walls of the mansion in frozen muteness, as the Aziz clenched his jaws, and gawked back at Joseph with fiery, condemning eyes.

"Joseph?"

Chapter Seven

"What are you doing here, Joseph?" the Aziz asked in an accusatory tone.

But what was there to say? He was caught with torn clothes in the Aziz's private premises, and his wife shaking in a revealing nightgown, covering her tomato-red face with her pale hands. Nothing about this scandalous scene screamed "innocence".

"Joseph? What are you doing in MY BEDROOM SUITE?!" he roared.

"What does it look like?" Zulaikha quickly regained her composure and took advantage of her husband's obvious suspicion. "This is the slave you raised in your own house and rewarded for his every word and action. What is his reward now? What's the reward for the one who has ill intentions towards your family, my master?"

"Is this true, Joseph?" the Aziz asked him under his breath.

Joseph stayed silent. He couldn't admit to a crime he didn't do, and yet he didn't want to humiliate the Aziz by telling him his wife was an adulterous liar.

"Your so-called 'son' barged into my bedroom while I was taking a nap. I begged him for mercy but he wouldn't listen! I tried to struggle to get him off me, but he covered my mouth to stop me from screaming out for help. That's the reality of the man you treated like family! You should lock him up for life and let him suffer the worst kinds of torture for betraying your trust this way after everything you've done for him."

"Is this true, Joseph?" the Aziz asked again angrily.

"No, your Highness, it is not true. She's the one who wanted to have an affair with me," Joseph finally said.

"He's lying! Save your honour and let him rot in jail!" Zulaikha yelled.

A number of the house servants were already starting to gather around, curious to know what the commotion was all about. The Aziz was starting to lose his temper yet Joseph remained strangely calm.

"Say something, Joseph!" the Aziz hissed. "What do you have to prove your innocence?"

"I only have my word, your Excellency. I don't know how else to prove it."

"Of course he will deny his hideous crime," Zulaikha exclaimed, then turned around to address the servants. "Does any one of you believe him? Can anyone here testify he's telling the truth?"

The whispers lowered with the rising tension. Even if anyone had seen or heard anything, no one would dare utter a word. What servant in the right state of mind would stand up to a woman like Zulaikha?

"I have something to say. May I speak, your Excellency?"

He was one of Zulaikha's cousins who happened to be visiting and staying as their house guest for a couple of days. He was known to be a very wise person, and after observing the whole incident, he felt obliged to help.

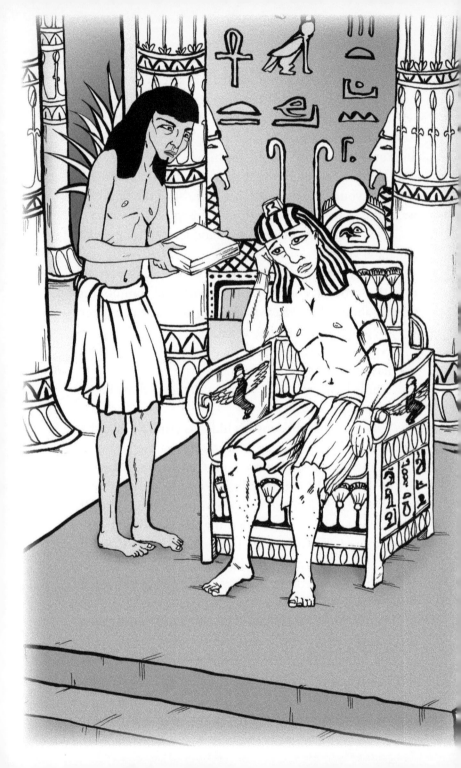

"If it happens to be the case that Joseph's shirt is ripped from the front, then she's spoken the truth and he is from the liars. And if it happens to be that his shirt is ripped from behind, then she lied and he is from the truthful."

Joseph turned around slowly and like a shrewd, faithful lawyer for the silently chaste victim, the shirt that once proved his brothers' guilt, confirmed the truth again to those who sought it.

"This must be the scheming of you women. No doubt your schemes are grave." The Aziz finally turned to his wife with a disappointed look then shook his head. She covered her face in shock and humiliation. He then ordered everyone to leave at once after warning them viciously to never speak of what had happened that night.

"You are an honourable man, Joseph," the Aziz said, patting him on the back stiffly like a calculated politician adamant to contain the damage. "I trust you will stay discreet about this and put it all behind you. Tonight, we will be receiving a huge delivery of cedar wood from Byblos, and I need you to go take care of it."

"Yes, your Excellency," Joseph said humbly before excusing himself.

"And you, Zulaikha! Seek forgiveness for your sin. I don't want you getting into any more trouble," the Aziz added before retiring to his chambers.

Nightfall cloaked the mansion with drapes of dark shame, as the master chose to become a slave to his high status, and his wife who had already become a hostage to her desires, shared the same bed in total silence, both jailed in their own sleepless nightmares.

***

Gossip spread around the city like wildfire the very next day. From servants eavesdropping to guards and commoners relating stories to high-class women hungry for scandalous rumours, everyone was talking about Zulaikha trying to seduce Joseph.

"Oh dear! The Chief Minister's wife has fallen in love with a slave!"

"She must have lost her mind!"

"He's young enough to be her son!"

"If she's going to cheat, at least pick a man of her own status!"

"Are you saying her husband found out and didn't do anything about it?!"

"What a disgrace! Seducing a poor slave and getting rejected!"

"I heard she's completely obsessed with him. She's clearly delusional."

"You'd think a woman this rich and beautiful could do better. How desperate has she become?"

Rumours and chatter travelled all around and landed back in her house, bearing humiliation and indignity. Zulaikha paced her room angrily, infuriated with people's blabbering behind her back. Some of those foolish, gossip-hungry women defaming her reputation were actually her closest friends! This was getting ridiculous, and pretty soon she would find herself the joke of the whole town. She needed to counteract them and fast.

"I will show them who Lady Zulaikha is! I will reveal their real faces in a way they can never raise their heads again from the humiliation," the Aziz's wife seethed, as she addressed her poor, terrified maid. "Send out invitations to all of the aristocratic women in the city. I'm having a huge feast and it will be a night they'll never forget!"

A few days later, the mansion vibrated with the sound of music and the extravagant ambience Zulaikha created for her privileged guests. Rugs from Persia, ebony and ivory pieces from African kingdoms, golden vases and sculptures from Nubia, and precious stones and gold ornaments were all displayed lavishly across the hall where the party was taking place. Servants clad in scant costumes carried trays filled with an array of different delicacies. The dinner tables were set elegantly around cushioned seating with flower arrangements and rich dishes of rosemary flavoured beef, duck stuffed with exotic fruits, goat meat sweetened with honey and mustard, and the best kinds of seafood. Plates filled with chickpeas and lentils, lettuce, and cucumbers were passed around before dessert. The women marvelled at Zulaikha's beauty as she walked in, wearing a long tunic embroidered with golden threads and an expensive long wig drenched in perfume and accessorized with unique, exceptional jewellery.

"Did you sharpen and polish the guest knives?" she asked the butler with clenched teeth, after welcoming the rich women with a feigned smile.

"Yes, your Highness," he declared with a respectful bow.

"Sharpen them again!" Zulaikha snapped back.

Dainty bowls of whole fruits were then passed around with special guest knives and glasses of the finest wine. It was at this moment, when all the women were seated, busily chattering and peeling their fruits, that Zulaikha called out for Joseph to enter.

"Goodness gracious! Is that an angel that just walked in?"

"He can't be human!"

"This is supernatural beauty! Who is this man?"

Zulaikha smiled triumphantly when she saw her guests bedazzled by Joseph's beauty. They were mesmerised to the point that some of them didn't even feel the sharp knives cutting through the fruits and slitting their hands. Their blood dripped on their fancy outfits,

and still their eyes were fixed on him, hypnotised by his unearthly charm. Joseph lowered his head in disappointment, avoiding the lustful looks of the rich wives, feeling humiliated and ashamed at how Zulaikha was showcasing him to her friends like a prized possession, especially when he was ordered to tend to their wounds, and more women started deliberately cutting themselves just so they could be near him. They gathered around him like hawks, surprised at his chastity and insistence to ward off their unsolicited attention. They were all over him, completely losing control of their sanity and proper public demeanour.

"We've never met anyone like him."

"He's an angel personified in an earthly figure."

"This man is Joseph, the slave you blamed me for seducing!" Zulaikha crossed her arms, feeling superior again. "What you heard is true. I did try to entice him and he did refuse and chose virtue instead. You saw him once. Only once! And look how overwhelmed you all became. Imagine seeing him every single day. What would you have done if you were in my place?"

The women fell silent. After all, what was there to say? They were still literally intoxicated by Joseph's magnetism. They were all in the same boat now, and should this reach their husbands, they all risked an unimaginable scandal. Zulaikha had artfully reclaimed her power once again, and every woman in the room knew it.

"Now," Zulaikha crossed her arms in the most superior manner, "I'm sure you all agree that I have all the right to be honoured and obeyed by my slaves. Joseph has no choice but to attend to my wishes, and perhaps even later on to my lovely guests' wishes, too," she winked evilly.

Joseph felt like a drowning man in the high waves of immoral behaviour. He was now the highly sought bachelor that not only the Aziz's wife desired, but also all of her distinguished friends. Even though he had it in him to refrain from their shameless invitations and suppress their barefaced innuendos, for any ordinary man, it would not have been easy to resist all those beautiful women.

The Aziz's wife ordered her servants to show the eager guests out and decided to give Joseph one last chance to surrender. Her husband left for Lebanon on an urgent business trip and wasn't scheduled to come back for a few more days. Any feelings of remorse or guilt Zulaikha had, she sent away in her husband's luggage. He let Joseph stay in the mansion after what had happened, which clearly meant the whole commotion of infidelity didn't bother the high and mighty Aziz, so why should it bother her?

Zulaikha approached Joseph with greater confidence; now that her little secret of debauchery was out in the open, she had nothing more to lose.

"I'm giving you an ultimatum, Joseph," she threatened in a calm tone. "Either follow me to my bedroom or follow one of those guards to prison. For life!

Chapter Eight

Locked inside the four walls of prison, Joseph sat alone in a corner in the middle of the night, watching all the other prisoners sleep in the confined spaces of their own anguish. It was ironic in a way; most of these people were here because of their sins, but Joseph chose prison to protect himself from committing one, and put his whole life on pause instead. He refused the Aziz's wife's corrupt stipulation and was sent to jail immediately with no trial, and no sentence clearly specified. The guard who shoved him inside the stuffy, dark cell told Joseph he would remain there "till further notice", and left with a sarcastic laugh.

Joseph was hoping that when the Aziz came back, he'd let him out and finally send him home to where he belongs, with his father and Benjamin. Sadly, for Joseph, his master condoned the unjust detention when he returned from his trip, and signed it off as a "crime of honour". It was probably his only option to stop all the ugly gossip after the party, he thought. But as the noble son of Jacob sat alone contemplating his life, sad memories of betrayal trailed before his eyes. His brothers' jealousy when they threw him in the well, the merchants' greed when they sold him as a slave, Zulaikha's wicked lust

when she invited him to sin, and her husband's selfishness when he knew of Joseph's innocence and still sent him to prison. In a world where all the right paths led to oppression, Joseph held on to his nobility, and asked the Lord to keep him strong.

Days dragged by as Joseph adjusted to his new life, making friends with his cellmates and listening to them pour their hearts out. His congenial nature ranched out like a beautiful green garden inside the gruesome boundaries of the prison, reflecting a positive attitude on the desperate men. He used his wit and wisdom to educate the prisoners the same way his father had taught him, years and years ago. He tended to the sick and lovingly took care of the feeble and old. He dissolved their quarrels in an atmosphere of affection that bonded them together as one family, freed from denunciation and superiority. Joseph soon became their leader and their trusted advisor in times of despair.

"You seem weary today, brother," Joseph addressed one of the prisoners, who once upon a time used to be the king's personal cook, before being accused of treason. "Is there something that's bothering you?"

"I am seeing the same recurring dreams and they've been haunting me ever since," the man replied miserably.

"I've been seeing strange dreams too!" exclaimed another prisoner, the king's former cup bearer. "Joseph, you seem like a pious, wise man. Perhaps you can help us interpret the meanings of our dreams."

"It would be my pleasure," Joseph smiled as he made himself comfortable and listened intently to both of them.

"I keep seeing myself standing with a loaf of bread on top of my head, and many birds eating from it," the former cook said.

"And I see myself pressing wine," the other man said.

"This is a sign of the wrath of god Apophis and god Horus!" assumed the wretched cook.

"Is that what my dream means too, Joseph?" asked the cup bearer. "Are the gods sending me signs?"

"I will tell you what your dreams mean before your food gets here," Joseph said confidently. "It's a talent my Lord gave me, the One and Only Gracious Lord. I have abandoned the religion of those who don't believe in His Oneness and in the afterlife, and I follow the religion of my father and forefathers: Abraham, Isaac and Jacob, who have never attributed any partners to the Lord! My friends, is it better to worship many different gods or worship the Only Eternal Lord? They are merely gods that you and your fathers have created, whereas the Lord's commands and judgements are for Him alone!"

The prisoners were dumbfounded by Joseph's words, for they had never been introduced to such thought-provoking revelations. Exploring the unfamiliar was frowned upon, especially for the poor servants who lived their lives obeying orders and doing what they were told.

"Well, that's just something for you to think about… now let me tell you about your dreams," Joseph continued, hoping his advice had turned a light on inside their hearts. "My friends, one of you will be the king's cup-bearer and make a living out of pressing wine, while the other will be crucified and birds will eat from his head. That's the answer to your enquiries."

Both men sunk into their own private silence. Even though Joseph didn't address each one individually, it was obvious the interpretation of their dreams meant the cook was going to die and the cup bearer was going to be freed soon. They both looked back at Joseph with admiration, while he continued to advise them on how to see life from a different angle.

"It was out of your gentle kindness that you never stated it to my face, but I know I'm going to die soon… I hope that one day your wisdom is put to use and impacts the world for the better," the former cook said in a hopeless tone.

"My friend, only the Lord knows when our time will be up. I translated your dream but it doesn't mean I can foretell the future. Don't think of when or how you will die; sooner or later we are all going to die. Think of how you want to live. Pass your knowledge forward and leave a mark on this world. Search your soul before you meet the Lord… In my heart I know you will find a life of timeless bliss and faith."

The former cook hugged Joseph warmly with tears in his eyes, and thanked him for his soothing words that swept across his sad fears like a peaceful breeze.

After a period of time had passed, the two men's dreams visited reality like awaited guests. The former cook was crucified in a public arena as people watched the birds pick at his corpse, while the cupbearer bid his prisoner friends farewell after finally receiving the happy news of his release.

"You are one special man, Joseph," he said, ready to leave for the king's palace. "It's a shame you're locked up here when you could have made a great difference in the outside world. You're truly one of a kind, and the time I've spent here with you has changed me in ways you'll never know."

"Take care of yourself, my friend, and remember to pass what you've learnt to others whom it might benefit," Joseph reminded him sincerely before bidding him goodbye.

"When will you be out, Joseph?"

"Only the Lord knows, my friend."

"You don't belong here. This is unfair!"

"Then maybe the first thing you should do when you're out of here is fight injustice. Mention my story to the king, and tell him how I and many other innocent men were thrown in jail unlawfully. Seek justice every chance you get, my friend."

"I will, Joseph. I promise!"

But the sad truth unfolded with time, for the devil has his deceptive ways in distracting people from pursuing upright morality, and swamping them with their own personal worries and concerns instead. The sworn enemy of righteousness blindfolded the cupbearer with forgetfulness the very same day he parted with Joseph. He went back to his job, leaving Joseph alone with his cruel destiny in prison for several more years, abandoned again with no one to stand up for him.

Far across the city, Zulaikha was in no better position; in fact, she became much more of a prisoner than Joseph ever was. No amount of fancy banquets or late-night temple visits could ease the pain of her wretched heart. Crestfallen and heartbroken, she'd become an empty shell, drained by guilt and grief. Many times she would send one of her trusted maidservants to go visit Joseph and knock some sense into him, promising him his freedom, but again Joseph would not be deterred, neither by threats nor by lavish lures. His rejection sparked her rage, making her order the prison warden to torture Joseph and whip him out of his spirits, yet again, nothing worked. His faith was too stern against her lust and revenge. Her life became a tormented nightmare, chained by depression heavier than the steel chains around Joseph's ankles and throat.

"It's a recurring dream, not just a random one! There must be a message or a meaning behind it," the king said anxiously.

"Relate it to us, your Majesty. I'm sure we can help you interpret it," his advisors said.

The king of Egypt was getting more disconcerted and restless by the day. Lately he'd been dreading going to bed at night, for he always had the same confusing visions, and he had absolutely no idea what they meant.

"I see seven big cows being devoured by seven skinny cows, and seven lush ears of grain wrapped with seven dry ones. What does this mean?" the king asked his men.

"Those dreams probably don't mean anything, your Majesty," his advisors finally agreed after consulting with each other. "Perhaps your stress is causing you to see nightmares."

"But why the number seven specifically? It's every single time! I'm sure it's a sign for something really important," the king argued.

"Forgive us, your Majesty, but we have no experience in dream interpretation," they finally admitted.

"Then find me someone who does! Now!" the king roared with frustration.

The search for the much-needed talent at that time yielded no contenders; there was not one professional dream interpreter, advisor, sorcerer, priest or even layman who could explain the hidden indications of the king's repeated vision. Panic raced across the palace as the king became impatient for answers, drowning his worries in alcohol every night in hope of dreamless sleep. His loyal cup bearer worked up the courage to talk to him one evening. After six years of freedom, being caught up with his job and busy getting back to real life, the cupbearer had a sudden jolt of realisation when he heard about the king's mysterious dream. He remembered the handsome, pious man who had once interpreted his own vision several years ago, the same innocent man he had once promised to help get out of prison.

"May I have permission to speak, your Majesty?" the cupbearer asked the king while he poured him another cup of wine.

"If it's another ridiculous guess or speculation about my dreams then I'd rather you stay quiet," the king snapped back.

"On the contrary, your Majesty. I have the final solution to your problem. I know a man who can perfectly explain your dream. He has an unusual talent! I once had a recurring dream myself, and his interpretation of it soon came true, and my friend had a dream that birds were eating bread from the top of his head and that same wise man told him his dream meant that he'd be crucified, which he was! I'm telling you, your Majesty; he's the one you're looking for."

"Then what are you waiting for? Call upon him at once," the king got up excitedly.

The cupbearer stated in a sad and quiet voice, "I'm afraid it's not that simple... he's in prison."

"Excuse me?!" the king's tone suddenly changed. "You think a common criminal is talented enough to interpret MY DREAM?!"

"No, your Majesty, he's not a criminal. The whole city knew he was innocent, even the Aziz himself was sure of his virtue when he threw him in jail," the cup-bearer said defensively, ashamed of himself for forgetting about his wise friend all this time.

"Then go talk to him and see if he can be of any assistance," the king said in a calmer tone. "At this point I'm desperate for any clues. Tell him I'll give him what he wants if he comes up with answers."

"Right away, your Majesty," the man hurried out.

The cupbearer felt a rush of mixed emotions as he boarded the fastest ride to the far end of the city where prisoners were locked up. How was he going to face Joseph after all these years? He was on his way seeking his help after he broke his promise to Joseph and let him spend precious years of his life jailed in a forsaken cell. He practised his speech before passing the gates, armed with the notion that the king had almost promised he'd free Joseph if he interpreted the dream correctly. That was good enough news, wasn't it?

"Good evening, Joseph," the cupbearer said to him carefully, in awe at how a lowly prisoner could look so noble after so many years.

"Good evening, my friend. It's been a long time. How have you been?" Joseph greeted him warmly.

"I know you must be upset with me, and you have every right! I broke my promise to you and now..." the man stuttered, trying to recollect his well-prepared speech.

"Don't apologise, my friend," Joseph smiled. "Destiny takes its course and the Lord's Will prevails. You're here and as a visitor this time. It means a lot to me you came back."

"In all honesty, I'm here with another motive," the cupbearer lowered his head.

"Then let's find a comfortable place to sit and talk, just like old times." Joseph took his hand and led him to his private corner.

"Joseph, your kindness is too much to bear. I don't deserve it."

"There is no blame here, my dear old friend, and besides, everyone deserves a chance. Remember that. Now how about you tell me what it is you needed help with… is it another dream?"

"Yes, but this time it's the king's dream," the cupbearer said, hoping Joseph would be impressed.

"What did he see?" Joseph asked calmly.

"He said he saw seven big cows being devoured by seven skinny cows, and seven lush ears of grain wrapped with seven dry ones. You've always been wise and sincere, my dear brother, so please help us interpret what this dream means. The whole palace is waiting for my return with any news."

"There will be seven years of prosperity in which Egyptian land will produce in abundance. This is what the 'seven fat cows' refers to," Joseph explained immediately to the anxious man. "That being the case, you should make great effort to plant as many crops as you can in those fertile years, to develop and enhance the revenue, and store the extra harvested crops in its ears. The seven years to follow will be years of hardship and drought, and this is when you should use the crops you have stored wisely to make sure they suffice. Then, after those seven dry years, a prosperous year will come with plenty of rain, and people will have enough crops of olives and grapes to make oil and wine, so be prepared to save enough of those seeds for plantation on the fifteenth year."

The cupbearer was stunned by Joseph's interpretation. It all made sense now! How did no one think of that? Not only did he explain the meaning, he also gave them a whole detailed plan on how to tackle the problem! The man couldn't wait to go back to the palace and win the king over with Joseph's refined analysis. He thanked Joseph warmly and ran for the door.

"Wait!" the cupbearer came back a minute later, confused. "You didn't state your demands or reward. You just helped the same people who have unjustly imprisoned you for years! You gave us all the answers with no conditions whatsoever! How is that possible?"

"Goodbye, my friend," Joseph smiled with a benevolent look in his eyes, as he walked the cupbearer to the door again. "Be good and take care of yourself."

Chaptër Ninë

"What else did he say?" the king asked, both puzzled and mesmerised by the perfect interpretation.

"That's it, your Majesty," the cupbearer shrugged. "I related to you every single word he said."

"So, this prisoner never demanded freedom first in exchange for the information? Or didn't even ask to meet with me to explain further details?"

"No, your Majesty. He gave me the full analysis and sent me back, wishing us all good luck!"

"Who is this Joseph man?" the king wondered. "He sounds too extraordinary to be a common criminal... Go back and take him out of prison. I want to meet him in person!"

The cupbearer followed the orders and went back with the release forms that the king personally signed for Joseph to be set free.

"It's the least we all can do for you, dear Joseph," the cupbearer said, his head lowered in shame. "You're finally free to go. The king genuinely appreciates your talent and wisdom."

"Did he sign my release papers because I helped him interpret his dream?" Joseph asked calmly.

"Of course. You were the only person in the city able to do it. The king was going insane with anxiety before you gave him the answer!"

"What if I didn't have that talent? Would he still have let me out?"

"Um, well, it's hard to say. He didn't know about you till recently. It was actually my fault that I never mentioned you to him like I promised," the cupbearer stuttered again.

"He's not sure of my innocence, and yet he's letting me out. Do you think that's fair, my friend? There are many men in here who were thrown unjustly in prison, and unfortunately, they don't have my talent to be set free. How do you think they'll feel if I leave now?"

"It's the king's orders, Joseph. He does what he sees fit!" the cupbearer whispered frightfully, looking around to see if anyone had heard Joseph imply the king was being unfair.

"If I'm being released as a favour or a reward for my services then I'd rather stay in prison. Do you remember how I told you to fight injustice? Letting me out with no investigation is a form of cheating."

"But the king has forgiven you."

"I don't need your king's forgiveness because I didn't do anything wrong."

"What are you saying, Joseph? Do you really want me to tell the king you refuse to meet with him?" the cupbearer panicked.

"Go back to your king and ask him if he knows about the noble women who cut their hands. Let him investigate the case before the final decree. I'll leave this place with honour and dignity and only when my innocence is proven before the whole city. Then, and only then, my friend."

The cupbearer left with a heavy heart and yet with deep respect for Joseph. Who would have that kind of patience and pride after being oppressed for so many years? Most men would jump at this opportunity! The cupbearer came back a minute later with a fearful look on his face, his eyes darting left and right with distress.

"What if the king roars so loudly that the whole palace stumbles to the ground?" the cupbearer asked, with images of the king's anger rolling before his eyes like a nightmare.

"Goodbye, my dear friend," Joseph laughed.

"I'm serious, Joseph! What if he gets really furious that you refused to meet with him and demands you stay in prison for life, or even worse, signs your death sentence?"

"Then I'll die as an honourable man with undeviating morals! I'll die knowing I lived trying to guide people to the truth..."

The king was shocked, to say the least. He was also very intrigued to find out what Joseph meant when he referred to the women who cut their hands. Everyone who knew of or witnessed Joseph's story back then was interrogated, until the king demanded meeting the Aziz's wife and her friends, and insisted he question them himself.

"What is the story of Joseph?" the king asked the ministers' wives standing before him in the palace hall. "What did he do when you solicited him?"

"He never succumbed to any sinful invitations, your Majesty!" one of the women admitted, relieved she could finally do the right thing after all these years.

"We know of no harm he's caused or evil he's done," another woman announced.

"He's always had the innocence and purity of an angel, your Majesty," said another.

"If that's the case, then why was he thrown in jail? And may I add, indefinitely!"

All eyes turned to the Aziz's wife, Zulaikha, who stood in the back looking drained with agony. Her beauty was stolen away by old age but mostly by overwhelming sadness over parting with her beloved slave, Joseph. She stood there humbled by her guilt and grief, accepting the accusing, penetrating looks that cut through her frail body like sharp knives. She knew she deserved it, even after she had wasted cherished years of her life torturing herself over what she had done to that noble young man who had grown up in her home.

"Today, the truth has been exposed," Zulaikha said, with tears in her gloomy eyes. "It was I who seduced him, and he chose chastity. He refused to betray the Aziz who trusted Joseph like his own son. I admit my mistake, and I'm not freeing myself from any blame now, for everyone here knows I deserve to be punished. We are all humans, your Majesty, and we all have weaknesses that sometimes incline us to do evil. Yet, I have faith that the One and Only Lord has accepted my repentance, for my Lord is the Most Merciful and All-Forgiving."

Zulaikha's bold confession took everyone by surprise. Was this the same woman who shamelessly told her friends she was planning to cheat on her highly esteemed husband with the young, handsome slave? Was this the same woman who gloated when the women cut

their hands with the sharp knives she gave them? Not only was she making no excuses and showing no signs of arrogance and entitlement, but she was also proudly and unapologetically affirming she had accepted Joseph's monotheistic religion.

"You confess you plotted against Joseph and you put an innocent man in jail!"

"That's right, your Majesty. Joseph is innocent."

"And is it true, that all of you women were so fascinated by Joseph that you cut your hands, and he paid you no attention?" the king asked her friends.

"That's true, your Majesty," they all replied.

"Why did you conspire against such an admirable, decent man?!"

"We ask your forgiveness...." Zulaikha said, her head bowed down with shame.

"MY forgiveness?! You should be asking for Joseph's! You took away precious years of his life, and for what? Your own whims!" the king roared. "Guards! Take these women to the palace's prison until I decide what I'm going to do with them. And bring Joseph here at once!"

From the small cell he'd lived in for the past nine years to the massive fifty thousand feet palace, Joseph walked down the halls leading to the audience chamber located in the south-east corner, where the king awaited his arrival impatiently. News of his innocence preceded his dignified steps on the beautifully painted floors depicting flowers, grapes, vines and fish. The walls of the chamber had floral patterns featuring birds and red and white calves, and wooden columns shaped as lilies supported the ceiling engraved with illustrations of beautiful goddesses. The king sat on his grand royal throne, eyeing Joseph as he walked in and greeted him cordially.

"I somehow understand why women would be mesmerised at the sight of you, young man," the king smiled. "And so we finally meet!"

"It's my honour, your Majesty," Joseph said, smiling back.

"I must say I've seen beauty, but it's nothing compared to what I'm witnessing now. Not only are you handsome, but you're also very perceptive, graceful and, may I add, utterly patient," the king admitted.

"Thank you very much, your Majesty," Joseph said.

"Your interpretation of my dream was truly remarkable. It reflects your wide knowledge and refinement, and if your speculation is true, then you'll be saving the whole country from a deadly famine."

"I believe the famine will not only affect Egypt, but many neighbouring countries as well. If we work according to the operational plan, we will be able to save the entire region from inevitable destruction," Joseph said in a confident tone of enthusiasm.

"What is your proposed plan?"

"The coming seven years will be a prosperous time for Egypt, therefore we need to seize that opportunity in the best and most efficient way we can. We need to work hard on planting crops, increase the production as much as possible and whatever we harvest will be kept in its ears to avoid decay from the extended storage time. I also suggest we store a special harvest of extra seeds for the fifteenth year when the drought ends and the Nile River flows with profusion again."

"I understand the number of cows in my dream

represent years, so do the ears of grain, but where did you get the information about the fifteenth year from?" the perplexed king asked.

"It's only a calculated assumption on my part, your Majesty. The pattern of seven years of richness followed by seven of poverty led me to believe the following set of years will be of abundance again. My God has bestowed upon me the gift of interpreting dreams," Joseph stated.

"So I heard correctly. You do not worship Egyptian gods."

"No, I do not. I worship the One and Only God."

"I respect that and I am enthralled by your intelligence and pragmatism. From this day forward, you will be my personal consultant, the king's personal aide. You'll be given full trust and freedom to handle the country's affairs in the best way you see fit, and you'll be held in the highest rank here in my palace!" the king announced proudly.

"I'm grateful for your respect and trust, your Majesty. But with all due respect, I believe I will serve the country better if you set me over the storehouses of the land. I will guard them with full loyalty and knowledge. It will help me perfect my proposed plan to benefit both Egypt and the surrounding provinces," Joseph requested humbly.

"Your request is granted! And I will make sure your orders and demands are readily carried out," the king agreed.

"Thank you, your Majesty. If you will give me permission, I'd like to start work right away," Joseph said before heading out.

"One more thing before you go," the king stated as

he approached Joseph, "there's an unanswered question that still lingers in my mind."

"Yes, your Majesty?"

"Why do you care so much about the people's welfare, when none of them stood up for you, when you were unjustly imprisoned and mistreated? Where's your rage and urge to seek revenge?" the king asked.

"They are the Lord's creation, and it's our mission to work for society's benefit without expecting anything in return. I don't see why the whole country should pay the price for one person's oppression. Holding grudges only leads to spitefulness and evil, your Majesty, and that is against my Lord's commands," Joseph explained in a solemn, wise tone.

"These can't be the manners of a normal human being. You must be an angel sent to us from a holy place. Who are you, young man?"

"I am Joseph…"

***

A grand ceremony was held in Joseph's honour before announcing him 'Treasurer' and Head of Agriculture of the Egyptian government. The King himself commemorated the celebration and appointed Joseph with the "golden position" amongst the nobility and state politicians. Zulaikha watched from a distance, smiling proudly while hearing Joseph's speech. Her husband, the Aziz, hadn't been feeling well since the day everyone was exposed, and couldn't attend the ceremony, perhaps out of shame more than illness. Joseph's request to free the ladies from prison did not help with the Aziz's guilt and embarrassment. He also requested that many of the prison inmates be freed, especially the ones he'd been in close contact with over the years and was sure of their conduct and potential. The king was eager to grant him all his wishes, and so the prisoners were invited to visit Joseph at the palace, and made part of his trusted crew helping him manage the country's affairs.

The wheels of time moved forward as Joseph's life took a huge turn. His speculation of the king's dream came true, and during the seven good years, he guarded the land's treasures and granaries with sincere loyalty and commitment. Joseph had full control over the cultivation, harvesting and the storage of crops, and was given full authority to handle all financial affairs in the way he found served the country best. Joseph made sure the labourers who worked from dawn till dusk were fairly compensated and the ears were properly stowed away for the anticipated drought. Living with the Aziz when he first came to Egypt had taught him a lot about the country's economy; he had absorbed every detail like a sponge, and was now improvising and implementing his knowledge with full passion.

One could not say the same for his teacher. For years, he'd been sick and bedridden, both with grief and anger. Healers and priests were coming in and out of his chamber, yet no one was able to cure the Aziz, who'd become terminal at this point. Whenever Zulaikha would come visit him, he would refuse to see her, until the day came when he was too weak to throw her out.

"I know it's too late... but I've come to beg for your forgiveness. I've been a terrible wife and if I could turn back time, believe me there's so much I would have done differently," she wept as she watched her husband take his last breaths.

At the luxuriant funeral of the Aziz, none other than the wise Joseph was appointed in his place as governor of Egypt, given his unyielding effort in the past years and the fact that he grew up in the Aziz's home and had surely benefited from his wisdom throughout the years. Although some people were not happy about the fact that a foreigner was granted such high power, once Joseph revealed his plans for surviving the drought years to the Egyptian people, there was no doubt he was perfectly fit for the job.

"Don't you ever rest, your Excellency?" the cupbearer asked him one evening after he came back from the fields.

"That sounded very formal," Joseph smiled. "Do you not consider me your friend anymore?"

"Things have changed, your Excellency! You're now the high and mighty chief, and yet you still work as hard as a labourer. You rarely rest or sleep, and you spend most of your time in the burning sun supervising the harvest while you can do it from the comfort of your royal suite." The cupbearer bowed.

"I'm still Joseph, my friend. Minister or prisoner or slave, people are all the same in the sight of the Lord, and it's our hard work and solid faith that raises us up to the highest ranks. I don't want you to ever bow that way to me again. Please!"

"Noted, your Excellency. All I'm saying is try relaxing a little bit, and enjoy your lavish life. You're being too hard on yourself."

"The ones prone to stray from the right path are those afflicted with superior positions and worldly treasures. Money and power can change people, and it takes a great deal of strength to maintain one's ethics in the face of temptation. I associate myself with the poor as much as I can to be reminded of why we are here," Joseph explained wisely.

"So why are we here?" the cupbearer asked, after a long, thoughtful pause.

"I'll let you figure that one out on your own, my friend," Joseph smiled before going back to work.

By the end of the eighth year, famine struck the region hard like a merciless firebolt, exactly as Joseph had predicted. The country faced a tremendous downfall of starvation. Men were robbing their neighbours' houses looking for food, children were crying day and night from hunger, women were collapsing with weakness and older men were giving up, laying themselves on the ground to die. Middle Eastern tribes flocked to Egypt seeking help from the only man who had planned ahead for the catastrophic economic crises. Joseph shined like a ray of hope in the darkness of scarcity, as he reached out his hand to everyone and anyone in need.

Despite his huge responsibilities and the stressful effects of the drought that took its toll on the country, Joseph still managed to host all the foreign delegates and welcome them to the palace one by one. He met with hundreds of people a day, making sure their stay was comfortable and their requirements were met. The new chief refused to watch the envoys turn to beggars; he treated the defeated Arab merchants with respect, and offered them food and grains in exchange for their stocks, as worthless or insubstantial as their goods may have been sometimes.

"You've done an astounding job, Joseph," the king

addressed him proudly. "For an economy that is highly dependent on agriculture, you still managed to turn the challenge of famine into a genius plan of growth."

"It's my pleasure to be of any service, your Majesty," Joseph smiled humbly.

"You're selling the surplus grain for a very small price though," the king commented. "I even heard you exchange the ears for cheap merchandise with those who can't pay in cash. What do you plan to do with all that second-hand waste?"

"I'm implementing a barter-deal to encourage people to work instead of complain about unemployment and raised prices. Our kingdom is blessed with reserved grain that would last us far more than seven years, but I'd rather people not depend on the surplus and stay idle. In addition to agriculture, we are now transforming Egypt into one of the most thriving trade zones in the Arab world, your Majesty!"

"I like your way of thinking and how you plan ahead, but I still don't understand how the barter-deal benefits our economy when all you get is useless waste!"

"In the past year, we have established a special department for recruiting the unemployed and used the surplus merchandise brought by foreign designates to put our people to work," Joseph explained to the eager king. "We have a whole assembly unit with varied subdivisions for categorising, reusing, manufacturing, and selling the new products. The Egyptian market is already booming in spite of the drought! Rest assured, your Majesty, what you see as useless waste is actually being renovated to deliver huge profits!"

"You are a genius," the king exclaimed. "How will I ever reward you?"

"Just knowing I contributed, with the help and blessings of the Lord, in saving people's lives during such a rough time is enough reward for me, your Majesty," the new chief replied humbly, before heading back to his premises.

The wise chief minister interviewed each and every group that came pursuing his aid, making sure the grains were being used for personal benefit and not for resale. He wanted to prevent any chances of monopolies in the neighbouring countries, which would certainly cause more harm than good. He distributed even measures of barley and wheat to each individual and encouraged them to use it wisely before amiably sending them home. His reputation for fairness and generosity echoed through the mountains people crossed to reach him, and they returned home with more hope for surviving the life they once thought was doomed beyond repair.

"Another group is here to purchase grains, your Excellency," one of the palace guards announced right after Joseph bid the Syrian troop farewell.

"May the Lord bless all the Arab nations," Joseph smiled. "Let them in please," he added politely.

"Good evening, your Excellency," a wretched looking man bowed with respect, followed by a number of poverty-stricken men. "It's our honour to finally meet the legendary Aziz."

"Have a seat, my friends," Joseph greeted them warmly. "You must have had a long, tiring journey."

The men sat down around Joseph with their heads lowered, humbled by the grandeur of his presence and his kind modesty. Awkward silence tied their tongues, like it did with all the former rich merchants who came to Joseph feeling helpless. The men were ashamed to admit they came bearing all their lifelong savings, which didn't even begin to cover the price of supplies they needed to buy. Joseph always took into consideration his visitors' feelings before their needs; he created a welcoming business-like atmosphere mixed with courteous hospitality to preserve his guests' dignity. He ordered the butlers to prepare dinner for all the travellers as he smiled warmly back at the men with knowing compassion of the hardships they must have been through to end up here.

"My brothers and I are very grateful for your generosity, your Excellency," one of them said when the food was promptly served. "We've heard all about your esteemed honour and kindness, but after what we've witnessed now, all of that great talk still does not do justice."

"Your modesty shows how much of a noble man you are," another one of them commented.

"We were a group of strong, undefeatable men. But the famine has beaten us down, your Excellency," the eldest one of them reminisced.

For a brief moment, the words vibrated in Joseph's head as the whole palace seemed to swirl around him in slow motion. The men's eyes and voices brought back memories he had locked up in a little box in his heart for many long, painful years. Joseph felt delirious; his heart pounded loudly against his chest as he stared back at his visitors. He fought silently for breath as he realised the ten men sitting beside him weren't just merchants seeking aid.

They were his older brothers...

Chapter Ten

Joseph struggled with mixed feelings of longing, sadness and relief as he strived to make light conversation with his prodigal brothers. Reuben, Simon, Levi, Judah, Issachar, Zebulon, Dan, Naphtali, Gad and Asher. It really WAS them! He searched their faces, watching them gulp down their dinner like starved wolves, absorbing the air that carried the scent of his dear country where his beloved father lived.

So many questions screamed out silently inside his wounded soul.

How is my dear father? Is he still alive?

Will I ever see him again after you pulled us apart so cruelly?

Where is Benjamin? Why didn't he come with you? Did he face the same destiny I did because of your jealousy?

Do you even know who I am? Has time purified your hearts towards me?

"Whereabouts are you from, brothers?" Joseph opted for casual conversation to silence his sobbing heart.

"We come from a city called Canaan, south of Palestine, your Excellency," his eldest brother Reuben declared in a miserable tone.

"I heard many people suffered through the unfortunate drought," Joseph said carefully, feeling his heart about to explode. "I hope your family and loved ones back home are safe and sound."

"It's been a rough year, your Excellency," Gad stated sadly, as he devoured the delicious food. From their tired looks, weight loss and modest clothes, Joseph could tell his brothers hadn't had a decent meal in a long time. That thought alone tugged at his heart more than all the pain he'd been through in the past. He couldn't wait to find out all about his father and young brother, which wasn't hard to do, given his eloquence.

"More bread?" Joseph asked his eldest brother casually. They all sat at the grand dining table in the audience hall. "So I understand all of you are brothers. Your father must be proud."

"We are the noble sons of a prophet, your Excellency!" Naphtali boasted, slurping down a big cup of soup.

"A prophet with ten sons. That's very impressive. You must have inherited a lot of wisdom and knowledge we can all benefit from." Joseph held his breath, waiting for a confirmation his father was still alive.

"Our father is still alive, your Excellency. He's back in Palestine with our youngest brother," Judah affirmed.

"Oh, so you're eleven brothers?" Joseph asked cleverly.

"Yes," Reuben blurted out before any of them could comment. "We left our desolate wives and children behind with our father and brother Benjamin, and came here hoping you would accept our inadequate fees in exchange for some food. Like I said, we are a big family, your Excellency."

They never mentioned anything about the brother they brutally abandoned more than thirty years ago, Joseph thought sadly. Why would they? To them, Joseph no longer existed. As far as they were concerned, he had probably decayed in the bottomless pit of a well. Not in their wildest dreams would they have ever imagined he was the same royal minister standing before them now, helping them out in a time of need.

If only they knew how the Lord works in mysterious ways…

"Why didn't your brother come to take his share?" Joseph asked indifferently, as he measured grain for them to take home in exchange for the meagre cash and merchandise they brought.

"Our father fears for him a great deal," one of the brothers replied in an offhand manner, "so he never lets him out of his sight."

"Your father will kindly have to make an exception this time, just like I am making an exception now. I'm giving you his share since he's an old man, but it wouldn't be fair to give you an extra measure for a young man who is not present," Joseph stated firmly.

"But, your Excellency, there's no way our father will let him come with us," Simon pleaded. "He'd never trust us with him alone."

"I beg your pardon?" Joseph asked, with one eyebrow raised.

"What my brother meant to say," the eldest one shoved his inarticulate younger brother to stop him from blabbering unnecessary information, "is that our father depends on our youngest brother when we are away.

He's an old man, your Excellency, and needs someone to tend to his needs."

"I believe you said you had wives and children back home. I'm sure they can take care of the noble prophet for a couple of weeks. The rules are clear; measures of grain are given out to each individual fairly, if not generously. With all due respect, I'll need to give your brother his share in person. I need a guarantee he actually exists."

"But, your Excellency, it's a little more complicated than you think," a profusely sweating Zebulon added with irritation.

"If I break the rule for you, I'll have to break it for all the other merchants or it wouldn't be fair!" Joseph stated firmly. "Bring your brother as proof, and I'll reward you with double the amount as a tribute to the noble prophet, and you won't have to travel back and forth so many times. But if you can't bring him here, I respectfully suggest you don't bother returning."

"Your request is our command, your Excellency," the eldest brother Reuben bowed to Joseph. "We will travel back and try to gain permission for him from our father. I assure you we will certainly return with our brother soon."

"Very well, then." Joseph shook hands with all of them before heading home. "Have a safe trip, my brothers, and please send my warmest regards to the noble prophet."

He couldn't stop himself from adding that last request. After all these years, a simple greeting was all Joseph could send back to his father, and it was all he could hold on to till they returned with his beloved brother Benjamin.

But what if they never come back? Joseph considered as he watched them gather their belongings and head out. They mentioned before that they had spent all their life savings in exchange for those measures of grain, and there was a big chance they'd be ashamed to show up with no more merchandise for the barter deal. Desperate for their dignified return, Joseph ordered one of his trusted servants to secretly place the purse with the money his brothers had paid into one of their grain sacks.

"I'll make sure to replace that amount from my personal funds." Joseph patted the confused servant after the job was done, and walked away silently to his suite.

He stared out of the window at the withered gardens that used to be blossoming and evergreen, lost in his own thoughts about how small this world turned out to be. Life played its very own little game, causing the mighty to fall and the downtrodden to rise up beyond the greatest expectations. The Almighty Lord promised victory to those who stayed faithful and patient, and standing here now after decades of yearning, seeing his brothers bow to him with defeat should have yielded a sense of triumph.

It didn't…

Joseph's tears flowed silently down his cheeks, feeling his heart ache with a burning to see his father again and take care of him. He had disconnected himself from his old life, fearing to cause disruption in the family if he ever found his way back. In these past years, he was content with the Lord's blessings, blocking out thoughts that his beloved father might have passed away. But today he was assured his family members were alive and well, and soon he would hold his father and Benjamin in his arms and they would all be reunited. Soon, he wouldn't be alone in this world anymore; he'd finally have a family to belong to and a place to call home...

Joseph, the poor slave turned royal minister with a twist of fate, cried alone in the privacy of his suite as he begged the Lord to keep him strong a little while longer, until that day came…

***

Onto the Jordan River Valley and back to Canaan, Joseph's brothers eagerly made their way home on their loaded camels, hatching up a plan of how to convince Prophet Jacob to let his youngest son go away with them. Memories of Joseph's pleading cries lurked in the desert while they discussed how to approach their father, given they were armed with the truth this time. Wolves hollowed on the moonlit path leading to their house, as they gravely avoided stopping by the chosen well where they had once cast off their innocent little brother. It was the forbidden subject no one was ever allowed to bring up again; no matter how many times Jacob beseeched and asked for a sincere confession.

Before they even unloaded their camels, the ten brothers hurried to greet their father and the rest of their families, and then asked to talk to him in private about an urgent matter. They weren't surprised to find him alone in his room praying, with Benjamin checking in on him frequently to see if he needed anything. Prophet Jacob had had a look of isolated sadness in his eyes ever since the harrowing night his beloved Joseph never came home. He held on to his patience like a drowning man hanging on to a raft amid the highest waves. If it wasn't for his continuing faith and whispered prayers, his heart would have imploded with grief many years ago. Believing the Lord would ease his pain and let him see Joseph again, and sharing his hopeful convictions with his loving youngest son were the only things that kept the prophet from falling apart.

"All we heard about the legendary minister turned out to be true," Issachar exclaimed, sitting down next to Jacob. "Not only is he very hospitable and generous, he's also unbelievably fair."

"It's good to hear country rulers are being even-handed during these harsh famine years," Prophet Jacob reflected.

"Yes, but look what his fairness cost us," one of his sons objected. "We were denied some supplies because you wouldn't let Benjamin come with us. The minister has strict rules not to give food for absentees."

"You'll have to relinquish some of your control, father. Benjamin needs to come with us to Egypt if you want this family to survive the drought," Reuben stated firmly.

"No!" Jacob replied in the same firm tone.

"Why not? You just admired the Egyptian minister for his fairness. Do you really expect him to give us Benjamin's share if he's not present?" his son asked.

"The minister clearly stated that if Benjamin doesn't travel with us next time, we shouldn't bother going back for more supplies," another son added indignantly.

"He's a grown man, father. Yet you're still overprotective of him like he was still a young boy!" Levi said heatedly. "Give us one good reason why he can't come after the chief minister personally asked for his presence."

"Unless you want Benjamin to starve to death," Asher remarked sarcastically.

"My answer is no!" Jacob said, getting up to leave.

"Father, wait! Please!" his eldest son pleaded, holding his father's hand to stop him from walking away. "Why won't you entrust Benjamin with us? I promise you we will guard him with our lives!"

"The same way you took care of Joseph?" his father asked cynically. "I trusted you with him. I trusted all of you! And you failed me miserably. My answer is no, son. I don't think my aching heart can take any more pain."

Jacob went back to his room to hide his hot burning tears from his sons' cold-hearted, persistent pleas. How could he trust them again, when they used the same phrases and made the same claims more than thirty years ago before taking his beloved Joseph away? They'd watched him suffer all these years and still no one cared to explain or soothe his heart with the truth. He knew his son was alive somewhere… every single time he heard someone walk through the door, Jacob's heart skipped a beat, hoping it was Joseph. Did his sons really think he'd forget about him in time? Did they think he would trust them with Benjamin after what they had done? He'd rather starve to death than see him go. Benjamin was the Lord's soothing balm to Jacob's pain; he was the light of his life. He was warm, kind and caring and lovingly took care of his father and wiped his sad tears away.

And in the hot burning heat of this drought that was killing people slowly, Benjamin was like a protective shadow that gave him comfort and support. He was Joseph's shadow, the shield Joseph left behind as a reminder that he would be back one day…

"Come in," Jacob wiped his tears quickly when he heard the knock on the door a little while later.

"If you will please allow me, father, I need to tell you one last thing before I go to bed," his eldest son said softly as he approached Prophet Jacob.

"Go ahead, son," Jacob said sadly.

"We were unloading our camels now, and look what we found in our sacks," the eldest brother remarked, putting forward a handful of money. "The kind minister gave us back the money we paid him for the food. He's a good man, father. A noble man like him would never harm our younger brother."

"I'm sorry, son, but my answer is still no." Jacob looked away sadly, after a long silence.

"It's us you don't trust, not the minister," his eldest son realised regretfully. "I don't blame you… Goodnight, father."

***

Weeks went by quickly in Prophet Jacob's house and his family ran out of food again, while the days dragged by slowly in Joseph's mansion as he patiently waited for his brothers' return.

"How are you feeling, Benjamin?" Jacob asked lovingly one evening. "You don't look well, son."

"I'm perfectly fine, thanks to the Lord," Benjamin replied with a smile, mustering all the energy he possibly could so his father wouldn't worry. The scarcity of grain was affecting his youngest son the most since he didn't receive his own share, yet still Benjamin never complained, and worked hard to make sure everyone else was comfortable and well-fed.

"Do you think I'm being unreasonable in refusing you to travel with your brothers?" Jacob asked sadly.

"I trust your judgment, father," Benjamin affirmed, "I just wouldn't want anyone to suffer because of me."

"We should leave for Egypt in the morning before completely running out of provisions," one brother said as he walked in, interrupting their conversation.

"I believe you have no other option," Jacob stated in a forlorn voice.

"May we remind you of the minister's warning, father. This trip is of no use if you don't give Benjamin permission to travel with us."

"The children are fighting over the food," one of the wives said, coming in unannounced. "Come eat what is left before it's too late."

Jacob went to the little dining area where his grandchildren cried and yelled over who got the last piece of bread. One of his daughters-in-law sat in the corner soothing her screaming baby, complaining she could no longer breastfeed him, while the other wives sulked silently, thinking of how they would be able to feed their children if their husbands didn't travel to Egypt to get some supplies. Standing amidst that scene, Jacob suddenly felt guilty and knew he would soon blame himself for his family's suffering. In his mind, he was sure that no harm would befall Benjamin unless it was already predestined by the Lord, and that his son would follow the tracks of his fate even if he locked him up in a high tower. In his mind he knew all of that and more.

It was his heart that couldn't take it…

"I will let Benjamin go with you to Egypt," Prophet Jacob sighed sadly.

"Thank you, father! You've made a wise decision," his eldest son smiled with relief.

"Yes, but on one condition!" the prophet stated firmly.

"Anything, father! Anything at all!" Judah guaranteed.

"I need you all to give me a pledge in the Almighty Lord's Name that you will bring Benjamin back home as safely as you took him," Jacob said, looking his eldest son in the eye.

"Unless we are all struck by some grave calamity, I give you my solemn pledge in the Lord's Name that I will not return home without Benjamin. I promise I'll bring him back safe and sound," the eldest brother swore, ashamed of his father's distrust and lack of faith in him.

"I will hold you to that promise, son." Jacob patted him on the shoulder. "The Lord Himself is the Greatest Witness."

"May the Almighty Lord be our Witness," all the brothers repeated with assertion.

"So if it's okay with you, father, we plan to leave at dawn," the eldest son added.

No matter how much they tried to deny it, standing there before their father like susceptible culprits needing to take an oath was harder than anything they'd been through since they got rid of their brother Joseph. Real men were held accountable for their simple words, but now their promises meant nothing to Jacob anymore. Their father needed an oath before the Lord. The ten brothers retired to their rooms silently, feeling disgraced, and vowed within themselves to not let their father down this time.

***

Dawn peeked into the family's house a little too early. Jacob held Benjamin tightly in his arms and wept softly. Even though he gave his youngest son permission to leave, the father's heart was desperately pulling Benjamin back to stay. The ten brothers walked in a little while later to say goodbye to Prophet Jacob, and found themselves lowering their heads with shame when they saw the sadness in their father's eyes.

Once you lose a loved one's trust, how do you gain it back? They all pondered silently.

"May the Lord guide and protect you, my sons. Have a safe journey and remember to separate right before you arrive, and enter the country through different gates. You're a handsome, powerful group and envious eyes might strike you with evil energies. Take your precautions, my dear sons, and let your hearts beat with faith in the Great Lord, for whatever the Lord commands will surely happen, and in Him we put our full trust."

"Will do, father," Reuben said as he kissed his hand. "And soon Benjamin will return to you unharmed, I promise."

"May the Lord return all my sons back to me safe and unharmed," Jacob prayed before saying goodbye to all of them.

"Uncle Benjamin?" his little nephew came running to hug him. "Are you going to travel with my father and other uncles?" the little boy asked sadly.

"I think I am, young man," Benjamin said, propping his little nephew on his lap.

"Don't go, Uncle Benjamin. Please don't leave," his nephew cried.

"Don't be sad, please." Benjamin hugged him warmly. "I'll only be gone for a few days. I need to bring us some food and supplies. Don't you want me to make you your favourite apple pie?"

"Grandfather Jacob said apples don't grow in the scout," the little boy sniffled.

"You mean 'drought', not scout!" Benjamin laughed. "Your grandfather is right, actually. Hmmm," he scratched his head pretending it was a huge crisis that needed a solution. "Then how about I go get the ingredients to make you my special olive bread?"

"And you'll still make a happy face on top?" the little boy asked, while wiping away his tears.

"I think I can manage that, your Majesty," Benjamin winked lovingly, hugging him tight.

"Take care of your grandfather for me, young man," he said before heading out.

"Take care of yourself for all of us, Uncle Benjamin," his little nephew said, with tears flowing down his pale face.

He must have rehearsed and pre-played this moment in his head more than a million times, but watching Benjamin walk into the palace with the rest of his brothers, Joseph fought back tears of happiness as he struggled to remain calm. His baby brother had grown into a handsome strong man, yet his eyes still had the same innocence and his face the same smile he loved with all his heart. Feelings of suppressed love and longing wrapped around the grand dining room where Joseph had a huge feast prepared for the men, a secret celebration that only he knew about.

The celebration of being reunited with his beloved Benjamin after more than thirty years of hidden grief…

"I finally meet the man himself," Joseph shook hands with his youngest brother warmly. "I hear your departure created quite a stir."

"I'm truly honoured and thankful to my father for giving me the permission to come here and meet you, your Excellency," Benjamin said politely.

"Your father is justified not to separate from you. A grown man who respects and listens to his father's word is an honourable man, Benjamin," Joseph smiled proudly, "Your name is Benjamin, right?" he added quickly.

"Yes, your Excellency."

"Everyone, please be seated." Joseph turned his attention to his brothers to escape any suspicion. "Let us have dinner together before talking business, my dear brothers."

The dining chairs were deliberately set in pairs, exactly like Joseph had requested. Knowing his family well, he knew his brothers would team up and leave Benjamin to sit alone.

"May I?" Joseph asked, pulling up the empty chair next to his beloved brother.

"It would be my pleasure," Benjamin replied in a desolate tone.

"I can't help but notice the sad look in your eyes, Benjamin," Joseph said in a voice low enough for his loud brothers not to hear. "Is everything okay?"

"Thanks to the Lord, everything is okay, your Excellency," Benjamin's tears started flowing. "I just suddenly remembered my brother Joseph. If he were here, he would have sat next to me and fussed over my food, reminding me to eat healthily and take care of myself."

"Where is he?" Joseph pursed his lips to suppress his need to scream the truth. If there was one thing Joseph couldn't endure, it was seeing his youngest brother sad.

"No one knows, your Excellency," Benjamin wiped his tears, fearing his brothers would notice he brought up the subject of Joseph after they threatened him never to mention it again.

"You have engulfed us all with too much kindness again," one of the brothers remarked, still chewing on a big morsel of wheat crackers. "We really don't know what to say."

"Say no more, brother. It's my pleasure to host the noble sons of the prophet," Joseph said amiably. "I've taken the liberty of preparing six rooms for you to spend the night. I'm sure you must be exhausted from your long journey."

The brothers gladly retired to the east wing of the palace where visitors were luxuriously accommodated. Seeing as there was eleven of them and only six rooms, Benjamin was again left to sleep alone while the others shared the bedrooms in twos. Joseph smiled to himself at the convenient arrangement, planning to come back later when everyone was asleep to pay his little brother a visit.

"Come in, please," Benjamin said when he heard the soft knocking on his door.

"I just came to check if the room was to your liking and if there was anything else you needed," Joseph said as he walked in and closed the door behind him.

"Thank you, your Highness. The room is perfect, I couldn't possibly ask for more."

"You know, Benjamin," Joseph cleared his throat, trying to sound casual, "I was thinking about our conversation earlier and what you told me about your brother. You never got to tell me what exactly happened to him."

"Like I mentioned before, no one knows where he is," Benjamin sighed sadly. "He went out for a picnic with my brothers one day and never came back."

"Do you think maybe your brothers harmed him?"

"I never said they did." Benjamin looked away quickly, feeling uncomfortable about besmirching his brothers to a total stranger.

"I apologise if I implied anything to offend you." Joseph couldn't feel more proud of his noble brother. "I'm genuinely sorry for your loss. You're a good man, Benjamin, and it would be my honour to replace Joseph, if you accept to take me as a brother."

"You're one of a kind, your Excellency. The whole Arab peninsula speaks of your greatness and fairness. You have been very kind and hospitable to my brothers and me, and we truly appreciate it. But to be honest, your Excellency, no one in this whole wide world could take Joseph's place in my heart."

"Well, I respect your sincere devotion to your brother," Joseph curbed his smile, his chest heaving, trying to remember the last time he felt this ecstatically happy. "My offer still stands if you ever change your mind."

"You do look a lot like Joseph, though." Benjamin knew it was rude to stare but he couldn't stop himself from gazing at the handsome minister. He suddenly felt his heart pound loudly when he saw the look in the minister's eyes and the innocent smile on his face. The resemblance was uncanny.

"I do?" Joseph asked slyly as he approached his brother slowly.

"I don't mean to pry, but can I ask?" Benjamin was perspiring and stuttering with anxiety. "Where do you originally come from?"

"I come from a faraway land where I used to spend my days with a noble prophet and a sweet little boy who loved apple pies."

Benjamin froze to the ground, feeling overwhelmed with a jolt of reality that was almost impossible to believe. He felt the floor slide from underneath him, and the room revolve around him at speed, making him feel dizzy and lightheaded.

"Joseph...?"

"My dearest Benjamin," Joseph embraced him warmly, with tears of yearning flowing down his face.

"Oh my Gracious Lord," Benjamin shivered and cried hysterically in his brother's arms. "Oh my Great Merciful Lord!"

"Shhhhhh it's okay, Benjamin," Joseph whispered, calming his brother down. "It's me, my dearest brother. It's me, Joseph. Oh how I missed you, young man!"

The brothers stayed up all night talking and laughing and crying about the past thirty years they had been apart. Joseph asked Benjamin about his father and how he had been doing all these years, and then told him about what his brothers did and what had happened in his life after that. Nostalgic memories soothed the pain in their hearts as they reminisced about the olden days and thanked the Lord for their merciful reunion. He finally sneaked back to his suite after Benjamin agreed to keep Joseph's revelation of his true identity as a secret for the time being. He promised he wouldn't tell his brothers, but when he got back home he'd surely let Prophet Jacob know he was right all along.

Not only is Joseph alive and well, he's also the highly esteemed royal minister everyone is talking about with respect and awe. Who would have thought…? Benjamin marvelled, closing his eyes. Feeling heavy with the events of the night, he fell into a deep and peaceful sleep.

"We can't thank you enough, your Excellency," Dan, one of the brothers, exclaimed the next morning after their bags had been filled with grain to take back home. "You've given us much more than our share this time. Our money hardly suffices in exchange for these generous supplies…"

"There is no need to thank me. I treat all of my brothers with generosity and respect. It's my duty to be of service to anyone in need at such harsh times. Just make sure you use your shares wisely, and may the Great Lord bless your food for you and your family back home."

"Again, we all thank you, your Excellency," Reuben said. "We should get going now as we promised our father we wouldn't be long. He will be impatient for our return."

"Have a safe trip, and please send my warmest regards to the Noble Prophet," Joseph replied respectfully.

Suddenly, and as the brothers gathered their saddlebags to leave, the court crier yelled out for the servants to lock the gates and not let anyone out. The palace guards surrounded the eleven brothers who stood in place, petrified and confused at the sudden unexplained arrest.

"What's going on here?" Joseph almost lost his temper

asking one of the guards why they held his guests back.

"These aren't noble men, your Excellency. They're thieves!" the guard replied.

"Don't you dare call us thieves!" Gad said indignantly. "Get your hands off me! We are the righteous sons of the Lord's Prophet. We only came here to do business, not to cause any trouble."

"What is it that's missing?" Zebulon asked curiously.

"The king's personal golden cup disappeared right when you people were busy packing," the guard said accusingly.

"There must be some kind of mistake," Joseph declared. "I demand you search the hall carefully before you throw out accusations."

"I had more than ten of your best servants search the hall, your Excellency. They still never found it!"

"This is ridiculous! We are not thieves, your Excellency," Reuben steamed.

Joseph stared back at his eldest brother silently, trying to read the expression on his face. It was a very awkward situation, and the guards were now waiting for the fair minister to investigate the robbery. Morbid silence swarmed the palace hall as the brothers held their breath, trying to escape the piercing, accusing eyes of all the people who quickly gathered around to witness the great scandal.

"Search our bags. We have nothing to hide!" Levi offered with assertion.

"What punishment do you choose for the thief, should we find the king's cup hidden in one of your bags?" the head officer enquired in a challenging tone.

"According to our law in Palestine, whoever steals becomes a slave to the owner of the property," Reuben replied.

"Very well then," the officer approved. "If the chief minister agrees, we will apply your law instead of the Egyptian law which provides for the thief to pay twice as much the value of the stolen property or face life imprisonment."

"I agree," Joseph said in an almost inaudible voice.

"Search them!" the head officer yelled at his subordinates.

"Wait!" Joseph lifted his hand up to stop them from mistreating his brothers. "I'll do it myself," he added calmly. "My brothers, please set your saddlebags on the ground and take a seat. I'm sure there's a misunderstanding. We need to follow the routine before we let you go, so please bear with us a little while longer."

"Do what you have to do, your Excellency," Issachar said, feeling utterly humiliated by the position they were put in. "I assure you, you won't find anything that doesn't belong to us."

"I'm sure I won't," Joseph said, "and that's when I will have every single person here who accused you of theft apologising profusely, and then I will personally deal with them after you're gone," Joseph said firmly, staring back intently at the aggressive officer.

The eleven brothers watched Joseph search their luggage, starting with the eldest one's saddlebag. He examined each and every one thoroughly, as the crowd viewed the suspense scene with anticipation, desperate for scandal. Joseph seemed calmer when he was almost done searching and the cup was still nowhere to be found.

The last saddlebag he yet had to check belonged to his beloved young brother. He opened it with ease, his hand roaming inside it briefly as he saw his brothers' relief, mentally preparing themselves to leave with whatever dignity they had left.

At that exact moment, Joseph's facial expression suddenly changed into one of complete distress. He took his hand out slowly as the crowd gasped at what they saw.

Joseph looked down at his hand that held the king's golden cup, then slowly lifted his head up, his eyes meeting with his youngest brother's eyes in dark confusion.

"Benjamin…?"

Chapter Eleven

Benjamin stayed silent while all ten brothers glared back at him with disgust and shame. He didn't try to defend himself or even ask for forgiveness. His eyes were fixated on the ground to escape the look on Joseph's face. He heard his brothers' muttering insults under their breaths, waiting for Joseph to announce the final verdict. They were so sure of themselves that they picked their own punishment, and now there was no turning back, since their youngest brother with the deceivingly innocent face turned out to be a thief!

"Aren't you going to defend yourself, Benjamin?" Joseph asked, looking shocked and disappointed.

"I have nothing to say, your Excellency," Benjamin said calmly, his head still lowered.

"You have every right to be angry, your Excellency," Levi exclaimed. "We aren't at all surprised actually. He once had a brother who had stolen before, why should Benjamin be any different?"

"Shame on you! What a disgrace to the family," the eldest brother muttered.

They were referring to him, weren't they? Joseph thought angrily. He heard the resentment in their voices with his own ears and was filled with regret. His brothers hadn't changed; they were still lying and blaming innocent people, and most of all they were falsely accusing their own brothers instead of uniting together as a family. Their hatred, jealousy and gossip were far worse than stealing, Joseph considered silently, and only the Lord knows the truth of what we secretly hold in our hearts.

"Guards!" Joseph roared with agony, "Take him away!"

"Your Excellency, wait!" the eldest brother panicked suddenly, forgetting his secret satisfaction and remembering his oath to his father, Jacob. "Don't arrest Benjamin, please. We can't go home without him!"

"His father is a good man, your Excellency. He will die with grief if Benjamin doesn't return with us," another brother explained.

"Justice must take its course, gentlemen," Joseph said firmly, "You all witnessed for yourselves and admitted your brother was a thief."

"But we promised our father we would bring Benjamin home safely. Your Excellency, please let him go and take one of us instead," Simon reasoned.

"Take me, your Excellency. I'll pay for his grave mistake, just please don't take him away," Reuben proposed.

"Are you asking me to set the thief who stole the king's cup free, and arrest an innocent man instead? Is that the kind of minister you think I am?" Joseph asked, offended by the insinuation.

"You're a noble man, your Excellency, and we mean no disrespect or offence. We are put in a very difficult situation here. We can't break our promise to our father. It will devastate him! Take one of us as your slave and please let Benjamin go. You will be serving justice and doing a good deed at the same time."

"What do I tell my Lord after I punish an innocent man for a crime he never did? This is why the Lord laid down rules and laws, and warned us to stay away from sin, even if it was justified by a good cause. No, I won't disobey my Lord, even if it were for the sake of His prophet!" Joseph stated determinedly.

"I'm begging you, your Excellency," Reuben desperately went down on his knees, "Let him go, I'm begging you, and in return for your favour we will all be your slaves."

"Stand up and pull yourself together, brother!" Joseph demanded as he helped him up. "Men don't go down on their knees to beg another human being. Stand up tall and proud. You're the son of a noble prophet for God's sake!"

"I'd rather beg or die than go home and face my father without Benjamin, your Excellency," Reuben replied with tears in his eyes. "There's a lot you don't know... all we ask is please take one of us instead. Our father doesn't deserve this, your Excellency, he doesn't!"

"I wish I could help you for your father's sake," Joseph turned around to hide his own tears, "but sometimes lessons are learnt the hard way, and innocent people are the ones who end up paying the price."

"What can we do for you to change your mind, your Excellency?" Issachar bowed. "We can't fail our noble father, we promised we would guard Benjamin."

"There's nothing anyone can do against the Lord's will. You could keep or break your promises to protect your brother, but the Almighty Lord is the Most Merciful Guardian; only He protects, not you," Joseph explained wisely. "I wish you all a safe journey back home." He then motioned respectfully for them to leave.

It was a lost case. The minister was adamant about his fair decision and nothing the brothers could say or do would deter him from implementing the law. The ten men dragged their feet and heavy hearts outside the palace, leaving their youngest brother behind. Just imagining how Jacob would react when they returned without Benjamin made them want to give up on life and die. How was their father going to even consider the idea his beloved son was a thief? He didn't trust his older sons to start with and now, even though it was the truth, he would never believe their story.

The trust was gone, just like Joseph and Benjamin were gone, and there was nothing they could do to turn back time...

"You must be out of your minds if you think I'll return home without Benjamin!" Reuben was going insane with guilt and fear, despite his younger brothers' efforts to calm him down.

"We tried everything we possibly could to save Benjamin, but he committed an unforgivable crime! Of course the minister detained him. He's a thief!" Judah gloated indirectly.

"An unforgivable crime you say?" Reuben scoffed. "And what we did to little Joseph wasn't? We threw him in a well to die, for heaven's sake!" he roared.

"In case your memory is dwindling, big brother, it was your idea to throw him there!" Zebulon spit out.

"You people wanted to kill him! I just wanted to get

rid of him to win my father's heart. So don't pretend it was my fault alone."

"Killing him would have certainly been more merciful than leaving him to rot alone in the dark!" Gad yelled back.

"Enough!" Asher put his hands up for a time out. "Why is this about Joseph all of a sudden? It's Benjamin we are talking about now."

"Don't kid yourself," the eldest brother buried his face in his hands. "It has always been about Joseph. Our lives have become an endless nightmare ever since we hurt him that night. Let's face it. What we did was inexcusable, and this is the Lord's punishment for all our evil deeds."

"It's getting late," Naphtali sighed. "Let's discuss this on our way home."

"I said I'm NOT GOING HOME!" Reuben steamed out with anger. "I can't face our father after I gave him an oath in the Lord's Name, I just can't! I'm staying right here and I won't return unless he gives me permission to do so, or the Lord decides our destiny, for He is the Best Judge."

The nine remaining brothers departed after losing hope in their eldest brother or Benjamin returning with them. Despair chased their tracks like a dark cloud as they prepared themselves to explain their brother's absence, hoping this time Jacob would believe them. Reuben stayed behind, and Joseph was kind enough to let him stay at the tavern attached to the royal palace, secretly making sure he was well cared for. In the meantime, Benjamin stayed inside the palace after the whole fiasco was put to rest, and that evening he and

his brother had quite an interesting private conversation.

"You could have just told me you came here looking for gold not grain," Joseph informed his brother with his arms crossed.

"Who would have thought my older brother was such a good actor?" Benjamin laughed.

"Well, you're not so bad yourself! Except for the part when you had your eyes fixed on the floor. What was that about?" Joseph joked.

"I couldn't possibly lift my head up. You were being so dramatic I was scared I'd ruin the act by laughing."

"I don't find this funny anymore, Benjamin," Joseph's tone changed suddenly. "I'm praying to the Lord our father takes this well, and holds on to his patience a little while longer."

"Don't worry about the Lord's Prophet, Joseph. Like I told you last night, our father is much stronger than everyone thinks. I've lived with him all these years, and I know his faith weighs more than all of the world's mountains put together."

"I just hope he forgives me when he finds out my true intentions..." Joseph pondered sadly.

The plan the two brothers had plotted the previous night worked perfectly, and now all they had to do was wait patiently for further news. After Joseph had ordered one of his trusted guards to hide the king's golden cup in Benjamin's bag and then arrest all the brothers for suspected theft, he made sure the officer would lure the men into choosing the thief's punishment instead of being forced to apply the Egyptian law.

"But how do I do that, your Excellency?" the confused officer asked.

"Work it into the conversation right when they start denying they're thieves. Take my long silence as a cue to ask them what they see as the most appropriate punishment for robbery," Joseph encouraged him.

"Why can't we just apply our own law?" the officer asked, even more confused.

"Because our law provides for imprisonment or a huge fine, and neither option will serve my aim. It's for a good cause though, trust me."

"Your wish is my command, your Excellency," the officer shrugged.

"Thank you," Joseph smiled. "Yes, and one more thing, if I'm a little aggressive with you for accusing my guests of theft, please don't take it personally. We both know it's all an act, right?"

At dinner time, and after all the other merchants seeking aid had left, Benjamin couldn't help noticing that his brother had a vacant expression, hardly eating or talking much. He knew this wasn't easy for Joseph, worrying about his beloved father's reaction, but what he still couldn't understand was why Joseph plotted this whole incident in the first place. He didn't have much time to explain his intentions last night, and he wasn't sure if now was a good time to ask him.

"Can I be honest with you, Joseph?" Benjamin toyed with the leftover food on his gold engraved plate, "as much as I try not to think about it, I'm still genuinely hurt and offended that my own brothers could believe I would steal. They even accused you of being a thief too. They haven't seen you in more than thirty years and yet they managed to insult you right to your face."

"They don't know I'm their brother, Benjamin,"

Joseph sighed sadly, still willing to give his elder brothers an excuse.

"That's when I was about to lose my temper and scream out the whole truth. Our father did not raise us to insult one another and throw false accusations! He taught us to protect family ties and stick together like branches; one alone can easily be broken but a bundle is almost impossible to break."

"Exactly! And that's why I'm glad you didn't lose your temper. Benjamin, you don't understand. I'm not trying to get back at my brothers for what they did; I'm trying to teach them a lesson they will never forget. Sometimes we need cunning wit to resolve a conflict, and it's obvious from what we both saw this morning that our brothers' hearts are still not yet purified towards us, especially towards me. If it were anyone else maybe I wouldn't have taken that extra measure, but these are our brothers, Benjamin. They're family! And we must never ever give up on family."

"Do you think in a couple of days they'll be able to learn a lesson they never learnt in decades?"

"I believe true repentance from the heart can do wonders to a person, even after years of sin."

"You're an amazing man, Joseph," Benjamin admired.

"Oh, that's a nice compliment coming from a thief like you," Joseph joked, with a twinkle in his eye.

"Do you think they'll come back for me?" Benjamin asked hopefully.

Joseph paused for a second. "I think it's time to pray and go to bed, young man," he quickly changed the subject.

The truth was, Joseph didn't know how sincere his brothers were, and if that harsh incident shook something inside their souls. All he knew is one should have faith in people, regardless of the harm they've caused in the past, and just hope for the best…

***

Back in the city of Canaan, the nine brothers dreaded the inevitable confrontation with their father, who was counting the hours until their safe return. They fought and argued about who should be the one to explain the unfortunate incident to Prophet Jacob. Since their eldest brother wasn't present, someone else had to volunteer for the undesirable job.

"Good evening, father," Zebulon mumbled nervously.

"Oh thank the Lord for your safety, my dearest sons," Jacob hugged him, then his eyes darted across the room looking for his youngest son and reading the expressions on his sons' faces. "Where is Benjamin?" Jacob's smile suddenly faded away.

"He's alive and well, father," Simon blurted out, "He just couldn't come home with us."

"What do you mean 'couldn't come home'?" Jacob sounded both confused and frightened.

"Your son is a thief," Levi spat out angrily, shocked by his own tone of voice. "I'm sorry, father," he then added in a lower voice, "but that's the truth."

"He stole the king's golden cup. The minister arrested him and took him away," Gad said sadly. "We pleaded with the minister to let him go and take one of us instead, but he refused."

163

"Ask the travellers who came back with us. Or all the neighbouring villages. They will confirm we are telling you the truth."

"We know we gave you an oath, father," Issachar finally said, with his head lowered, "but there was no way we could have foreseen the future, and we swear we tried our best to fulfil our promise, but it was out of our hands."

"Father, please say something," Asher begged tearfully.

Jacob's silence slit through their hearts like cold knives. He stared back at them for a long time, and then suddenly held on to the nearest chair to stop himself from falling. His knees weakened from the weight of his heavy, aching heart as he slowly sat down to absorb the shocking news. Only the Lord knew that snatching his heart out of his chest would have been less painful than what he was feeling now. He closed his eyes and whispered a prayer for patience, his hot burning tears flowing slowly down his pale cheeks. His sons watched him silently, wishing they could magically disappear or turn to lifeless statues to escape this crucifying moment of suffocating guilt and heartbreaking sadness…

"Father…?" Simon went down on his knees, hoping his father would scream or yell or say anything that might numb this throbbing pain they all felt inside.

"Your inner souls have betrayed you, my sons," Prophet Jacob finally said in a mournful tone. "I'll hold on to my patience. Maybe one day the Lord will bring all my sons back to me. Only He is All-Knowing and All-Wise."

He struggled to get up and then slowly walked back to his room, stopping for a brief moment to turn and look his sons in the eyes. "My son Benjamin is not a thief," he said confidently before closing the door behind him.

Locked alone between the four walls of his grief, Jacob sobbed rivers and oceans of agonising tears, thrashing like a drowning man to hold on to the raft of patience. He thought about his beloved son Joseph, allowing himself to grieve his loss, for since that volcano erupted in his heart the day Joseph never came back, his misery had started flowing like boiling lava eating at his heart slowly. Now he could no longer suppress his pain. Jacob's sadness was gradually staining his vision with a morbid darkness. He struggled to breathe, unaware that one of his sons walked in after his soft knocking on his father's door went unanswered.

"Father, please don't torment yourself this way," Dan cried.

"Leave me alone, please." Jacob looked away sadly.

"You are a noble prophet. Holy revelations have descended unto you and you have guided and taught so many people. Why are you destroying yourself this way, dear father? Where is your strength and faith?" his son reprimanded gently.

"Criticizing and rebuking me politely will not lessen my grief, son. I am the Lord's prophet but I'm also a human being with feelings. If it wasn't for my faith and patience, I would have died from grief a long time ago. I would have fallen sick or dropped dead the day you took Joseph away."

"For God's sake, father! You will never forget about Joseph or stop talking about him, will you? You will constantly mourn him till the day you die, even though it's been decades."

"I only complain of my sorrow to the Merciful Lord. I know from the Great Lord what you don't know," Jacob broke down crying, unable to hide his sadness from his son.

"Look at me, father. Look me in the eyes and see if I'm lying about Benjamin," his son said heatedly. "Don't think we are all not dying inside too. It kills me that you don't believe us! Look at me, please."

"Light some candles, son. I can hardly see my own hand," Jacob said as he wiped his tears.

His son looked around his father's room in confusion. The full moon lit up the place and there were a couple of lit candles shining brightly. Jacob's son moved the cup holding one of the candles closer to his father, feeling his heart beating faster with an unexplained fretfulness.

"Is this better?" Dan asked hopefully.

"I still can't see anything," Jacob rubbed his eyes and tried to focus again.

"The room is brightly lit, father. Your eyes just probably hurt from crying too much."

"No, son," Prophet Jacob opened his eyes and stared into space, "I think my vision has gone…"

Chapter Twelve

"No! Father, no!" Joseph woke up in the middle of the night sweating and shivering. He panted heavily as he looked around his royal suite and realised he was having a nightmare. He closed his eyes again and tried to go back to sleep, but the uneasy feeling that consumed his heart refused to let him go.

A few harsh weeks later, while Prophet Jacob's whole household suffered silently, it was time to go back to Egypt again for more supplies. The years of drought were draining the family members out of their will to survive, and with Jacob's blindness staring his sons right back in the face, it was hard to feel anything but guilt and hopelessness. The men had been beaten, and their father's silence was even more heartbreaking than their children's cries from hunger.

"We are all set to leave, father," Judah declared miserably, "Our wives will take good care of you while we are gone. Don't hesitate to ask them for anything you need. Anything at all!"

"There is only one thing I need, Judah," Jacob reached out his hand to hold the son he could not see. "I need you to never give up hope on bringing your brothers back."

"Joseph is gone, father! Benjamin has become a slave to the minister. And your eldest son refuses to come home. I know your heart aches for them, and if there was anything any one of us could do to ease your pain, we swear by the Lord we would do it. But we need to be realistic here! It would take an actual miracle for them to come back."

"Only the disbelievers despair of the Lord's mercy. I will continue to have hope for as long as I live. Go back to Egypt and enquire about your brothers. Hold on strong to your faith, my sons. Hope opens a new door when you feel like the walls are closing in on you. Have hope and faith in the Almighty Lord."

The nine men kissed their father's hand and took off to obey his orders. Nostalgic memories roamed the streets as they passed through the city gates to pick up their eldest brother from the tavern before going to see the minister. He looked miserable and worn out, his eyes swollen from lack of sleep. He sat in the corner on the floor, his food untouched and his head in his hands, sobbing silently. Where was the strong, proud man who took matters into his own hands? Where were the sharp, hurtful comments and evil challenges? The brother, who was once their leader, had been reduced to a little lost child needing a helping hand to find his way home. Nothing mattered to any of them anymore; their money and trade had vanished, their wives and children were back home sick and starving, their half-brothers were lost to them, their mistakes had caused their father to go blind, and most of all, their dignity and self-worth had been cast away in a bottomless dark well of endless guilt.

The sad truth was that death would have been more merciful…

"What did father say?" Reuben lifted his head up sadly.

The brothers paused for a long time then one of them finally said, "He said 'don't give up hope.'"

"Did he forgive me? How did he react to Benjamin's news?"

"He is holding on to his patience," Issachar said tearfully.

"If only he could see me now," Reuben said regretfully, "If only he could see how sorry I am, and how I'm getting the punishment I deserve."

The brothers broke down hysterically, unable to contain their feelings any longer. Their father will never be able to see their tears again, he'll never be able to see his sons' faces, or watch his grandchildren grow. It tugged at their hearts that Prophet Jacob's last visual memory of them was the day they came home defeated; the day they broke their promise to him and came home without Benjamin.

"What happened to my father?" Reuben got up suddenly, startled and shocked by their hysterical cries. He grabbed one of his brothers by the collar and roared angrily in his face. "What happened to MY FATHER?"

"He lost his sight crying over Joseph and Benjamin," Judah sobbed, wishing his eldest brother would kill him and put his heart at rest. "We explained what happened but we couldn't ease his pain."

Reuben eased his grip on his collar slowly, feeling the world collapse around him in a dark haze. His face turned pale with anguish and shock, feeling his knees weaken and his heart about to stop. His whole life flashed before him like smoky ghosts as he stumbled to the ground. He covered his ears to escape the sound of little Joseph in the well screaming for help, the sound of Benjamin crying at night missing his brother, the voice of his father pleading to know the truth, the fear in his voice when he let Benjamin go with them to Egypt, and the echoes of his brothers' guilty cries that were driving him insane.

Was it all worth this harrowing pain...?

"Take me to the minister," he finally said, still covering his ears and staring blankly at the wall. "It was we who were blind, my brothers. Our father lost his sight but his insight has never diminished. If he still has hope, then by God so should we. Let's go!"

Joseph was in a meeting with his subordinates going through the state finances when one of the guards informed him a group of ten men from a city called Canaan in Palestine were there to see him. He excused himself quickly and hurried to the audience hall where he usually met his guests. He had been struggling with a heaviness in his heart since that night he had a nightmare of his father, and today the time had finally come to hear any news about him. He hoped and prayed it was reassuring news.

"Welcome, my dear brothers," Joseph said courteously, inviting the men to be seated. "I hope the Lord's dear prophet is in good health."

The ten men stared back at the royal prominent figure standing before them feeling low and humiliated. Their shabby clothes and unkempt appearance contrasted strikingly with Joseph's majestic, silk outfit and groomed look. His alluring perfumed scent swayed across the hall elegantly, conflicting with their sweaty, dusty odours. However, his humble smile overcame their diminished pride and lost dignity. They came to him with nothing to offer, and so much to ask for, their backs bent with guilt and sadness, and their eyes lowered, filled with tears of shame.

"Distress has seized us and our family, your Excellency," one of the brothers admitted. "Our lives have fallen apart, and we come to you today with cheap, worthless merchandise and nothing else but hope for your charitable kindness."

Joseph could tell from the looks on their faces that something was horribly wrong. This was more than an unfair barter deal and begging for charity. His heart told him something bad had happened. Joseph's heart never lied.

"Please don't worry about the grain measures. You will be granted shares enough for you and your family back home. As long as you brought something to give in exchange, that's all that matters." Joseph then cleared his throat, "So how is your family doing? And how is the noble prophet? I hope he's in good health."

"They're surviving. Your Excellency, I know we are in no position to ask for any more favours, but can we please see Benjamin?" the eldest brother couldn't bring himself to talk about his father's condition just yet.

"We know slaves probably don't get visitors, but we seek your kindness again to let us sit with him for a brief moment, if that's okay with you, your Excellency," Simon pleaded.

"The noble son of the prophet is no slave!" Joseph

said proudly. "Rest assured, Benjamin is treated with honour and respect in this palace, and he has proved himself to be a valuable asset to this kingdom. Your brother is a very smart, honest young man, and everyone here treasures his fair opinions and shrewd perception."

"We thought since you found the king's golden cup in his sack, he would be regarded and treated as a thief. We saw and heard how you commanded the guards to arrest him," Levi said, confused by the minister's previous comment.

"Don't believe everything you hear, and half the things you see, my brother," Joseph smiled slyly.

"Our father was right," Zebulon realised slowly, "Benjamin didn't steal anything, did he?"

"No, he didn't." Joseph shook his head, finally seeing a positive transformation in his brothers.

"Then why did you detain him, your Excellency?" Gad voiced everyone's confusion.

"You will find out soon enough." Joseph's face lit up with happiness. "First, I have a personal request of my own. I kindly ask you to go back and bring the noble prophet here to the palace. I'd like him to see for himself how well his son is doing after all this time."

"Sadly, that day will never come, your Excellency," the eldest brother said with tears rolling down his face.

"What do you mean?" Joseph felt a sudden thud in his heart.

"Our father lost his sight, crying over Benjamin and his other lost son."

Joseph felt tears sting his eyes while he watched his brothers cry painfully from the gravity that struck their lives like an endless earthquake. He couldn't feel anything but numbness. He rested his elbows on his knees and put his palms together, feeling he could crush the whole world with his bare hands. He stared at the floor for a long time, breathing in and out slowly to absorb the dire news.

"We had a half-brother who passed away a long time ago," Naphtali admitted sadly, "so Benjamin's absence brought back many painful memories. Our father couldn't take it. He broke down reliving the loss of his son."

Joseph remained quiet, lost in sadness and shock. He finally spoke in an agonised, low voice. "Do you remember what you did to little Joseph?" he asked, still staring at the ground.

Morbid silence over filled the palace hall. The faintest sound would have been clearly heard in such muteness. Invisible blindfolds were taken off with a swiftness of sudden realisation, as the brothers finally regained their insight. The moment of confrontation they never thought they'd ever face was wrapping around them like chains of steel, and they finally realised the true identity of the royal minister when he lifted his head up again.

"Do you know what you did to Joseph and Benjamin, my dear brothers?" Joseph looked them in the eyes, unable to stop his innocent tears from falling down his face.

Benjamin's footsteps echoed in the grand hall. He walked in to stand by his brother, clad in a silk colourful gown that reflected the light from his bright face. Joseph got up to greet him silently, putting a gentle hand on his shoulder. He smiled sadly at his youngest brother, and then turned to the ten men who were still staring back at them in utter shock.

"Could this be true?" the eldest brother stood up, feeling he was about to lose grip on his sanity. "You are..."

The royal minister looked at them with a mix of pain, joy and relief and then finally said in a low voice, "I am Joseph."

Reuben took a step back, fighting for breath. The rest of his brothers gasped in shock. Joseph's elder brothers, who once gathered to strangle the little scared boy, stood frozen in place before him, now shivering with fear and regret. Memories came back to life as they witnessed what the future held for the young boy they were desperate to torment and get rid of. All this time, he treated them with respect and welcomed them to the palace like dear guests, giving them more than their shares and throwing feasts in their honour. All the times he enquired about Jacob's health, he was enquiring about his own father, and all the times he called them "my dear brothers", he was actually hinting at his true identity.

"I am Joseph," he confirmed gently, putting his arm around his young brother, "and this is my brother, Benjamin. The Lord has been Gracious to us, the way He promised to reward those who fear and worship Him with obedience, goodwill and patience. The Lord never lets good deeds go unrewarded, for He is the Most Fair and the Most Merciful."

The men's hearts reached up to their throats with terror and shame, and their eyes darted back and forth, trembling with fear like sheep about to be slaughtered. They stuttered, trying to speak, but what was there to say? Sins upon sins had been building up for over thirty years. They'd wronged their youngest brothers when they

should have been taking care of them, and caused pain to their parents when they should have been soothing them. They had gone astray, forgetting about the Lord who never lets tyranny win, and lifts up His oppressed creations with glorious victory in the end, even if they are cast in a deep dark well with no chance of survival.

"Do you know what Joseph has been through all these years?" Benjamin cried out. "How much he's suffered? How many years he'd been enslaved and imprisoned and tortured? Do you see what your evil jealousy has done to our family? To our father?! What kind of cruelty do you hold in your hearts?"

"Calm down, Ben..." Joseph said.

"He's right," Levi confessed. "He's actually being kind given what we've done."

"I have already forgiven you."

"We don't deserve your forgiveness..."

"The Lord has raised you above us, Joseph," Reuben admitted between sobs of regret. "I now understand why God has preferred you, my noble brother. Instead of honouring and standing by you, we were jealous and spiteful! Our jealousy blinded us and caused us to take the wrong path. Lord knows we have sinned, and we have nothing to say to defend ourselves. Whatever punishment you choose for us, I assure you will never be enough."

Joseph walked up to his eldest brother and slowly reached out to lift his chin up. He wiped his tears and smiled back at him with warm, sympathetic eyes.

"No reprimands or reproaches between us today," Joseph said softly. "We are one family, and I truly forgive you from the heart. May the Great Lord forgive you, my dear brothers. He is the Most Merciful of those who show mercy, and from your tears of repentance I can see you have returned to the right path."

Joseph hugged his brothers one by one, and let them cry on his shoulder while he soothed them gently with love and compassion. It was a marvellous reunion of purified and forgiving hearts that finally washed away the pain of the past. Forgiveness was a gift given to him and his loved ones, for his soul could not tolerate even the simplest ill feeling towards his family, his own flesh and blood. They were genuinely happy to see him, each one of them held him tight like they were scared to let go and lose him again. His plan to teach them a lesson had worked beautifully, and his unrestrained forgiveness had brought them closer together with no blame or criticism. The joy they all felt at this moment was worth all the pain; a moment worth a lifetime of unforgettable lessons and hardships they thought they'd never recover from.

"What about our father, Joseph?" his eldest brother asked with a hopeful tone. "How I wish he was here now. We have caused him so much agony throughout the years, and it breaks my heart that after we have found each other, he won't be able to see you or see how great you've turned out to be."

As much as he wanted to run back on foot to Palestine just to go down on his knees and kiss his father's hand, Joseph knew it was almost impossible to do that now. He was tied to Egypt with a huge load of responsibility, especially in those harsh drought years when he wanted to make sure fairness prevailed. Many people were already accepting monotheism and dutifully worshipping the one and only Lord. The Egyptians trusted him and the king depended on him heavily in crucial matters and important decisions, and Joseph was not the man to give up on public affairs and requests of the needy to tend to his personal life, no matter how much his heart was bleeding inside.

Joseph silently took off the royal cape of his outfit and then took off the shirt that was in direct contact with his skin. Benjamin quickly understood what his older brother was doing and asked one of the servants to fetch another shirt for the minister. She came back in less than a minute with a freshly pressed shirt for Joseph to put on. His brothers stood dumbfounded as Joseph handed the shirt he was wearing to his eldest brother.

"Take this shirt of mine and cast it on my father's face. His eyesight will return with the Lord's Will and Mercy," Joseph said, wiping the tears from his yearning eyes. "I kindly ask you to bring him to me. Bring your whole family if you can. I'd love to meet your wives and children. Benjamin has told me so much about them."

"Can't you come with us, your Excellency?" Levi asked.

"Your Excellency?" Joseph repeated jokingly.

"I can't help but think of you as noble in every way, Joseph," Levi said admiringly. "I only wish you could come see our father, just in case his sight doesn't come back, so he can at least touch you and hear your voice."

"Believe in your heart that God will give our father his vision back and it will happen, my dear brother. Faith is the most miraculous thing in this universe. It's the one thing we hold on to when we feel helpless against calamities and disasters. If only you knew how I wish to run back home to my father. But I can't! I'll have to stay patient a little while longer till you bring him here. He will see Benjamin, and me. He will! And his heart will be filled with joy, enough to erase all those harrowing years of pain."

As much as it was hard for the brothers to part with Joseph after that merciful meeting, they were very eager to go back home to Prophet Jacob and their families. The caravan headed back to Palestine bearing their brother's shirt and glad tidings of his blissful survival. If the ten men were wondering during their journey how they would explain that Joseph was alive, after repeatedly claiming that a wolf ate him many years ago, they never voiced their anxiety to one another. They'd been through much worse throughout the years, and they'd delivered more than their share of distressing news. This time, even though telling their father Joseph was still alive contradicted the story they'd been telling for more than thirty years, they were finally relieved to condemn themselves and let the truth surface if it would bring back their father's eyesight again.

***

Jacob was in a bad state. After his sons had left, he isolated himself in his room, refusing any communication with anyone but the Almighty Lord. His blindness had made it difficult for him to move around the house, let alone go anywhere else. His tears still flowed down his face day and night, and his prayers were the only salve for his injured soul. His life had become endlessly dark, with only his faith awakening a holy light in his broken heart.

"I seriously don't know what to do anymore," Levi's wife complained miserably. "The prophet hardly eats and won't leave his room to even play with his grandchildren like he always did. I'm scared that when the men come home, they'll blame us for their father's desolation!" she told the other wives.

"Prophet Jacob is a proud man," Reuben's wife retorted as she soothed her hungry baby. "Perhaps he feels he's become a burden on us after losing his sight. He'd rather spend his time praying and worshipping the Great Lord."

"Where are you going, son?" Judah's wife asked her little child, interrupting the women's conversation.

"I'm going to check on my grandfather," the little boy replied.

"Okay, but don't stay with him for too long. Your grandfather likes his privacy, so make sure you don't bother him."

The little boy nodded understandingly and went to knock softly on Jacob's closed door. He then walked in slowly, carrying a small bowl of stale bread pieces dipped in milk.

"I brought you some food, grandfather," the boy smiled. "I made it especially for you."

"Thank you, young man," Jacob wiped his tears and reached out his arms to hug the little boy, "but I'm fasting today."

"You're still sad about Uncle Benjamin, aren't you?" The boy sat on his grandfather's lap after putting the uneaten bowl of food down.

"We can't change our feelings, but we can control

them with our faith. I'm doing the best I can to stay patient," Jacob replied tearfully.

"I miss Uncle Benjamin. He's the best uncle in the whole world!" the little boy pouted. "He made me pies and played hide and seek with me, and he always told me the best bedtime stories ever."

"The same way Joseph took care of Benjamin when he was your age," Jacob pondered sadly.

"You mean Uncle Joseph? The one who passed away?"

"He didn't pass away! He's alive and well, and one day you will meet him, God willing, and you will love him just as much as you love your Uncle Benjamin."

"When will I meet him?" the little boy's eyes widened with curiosity.

Jacob didn't reply. He slowly put his grandson down and stood up, closing his eyes and sniffing the air around him.

"Grandfather?" the boy waited for an answer, confused by Prophet Jacob's reaction.

"Take me outside please," Jacob said suddenly, his eyes widening with disbelief.

The caravan was still travelling across the desert, approaching the prophet's estate with Joseph's shirt hidden amongst the grain. Jacob went outside to the living room where all the women and children sat together, waiting patiently for the men's return with some much-needed sustenance. He lifted his hands up to the heavens and smiled, still enjoying the scent he smelt in the air around him.

"You seem happy, Prophet Jacob! Are you feeling better today?" one of the wives asked carefully, shocked that Jacob had actually come out of his room with a smile.

"I feel…" Jacob lifted his face to the sky and closed his eyes again, "I feel Joseph around me. I can smell him in the air."

"You had to ask, didn't you?!" Levi's wife whispered, "He's obviously mentally weakened with grief."

"He will die weeping over his son Joseph," Simon's wife whispered. "What do we do?"

"We're worried about our husbands and our starving children and he's thinking about Joseph!" another of the wives hissed.

"You think I've gone senile?" Jacob asked the women, as though he could see the looks on their faces.

"No, of course not!" they all replied quickly. "Lord knows we are just worried about you. You keep holding on to frail strays from the past, causing yourself to live in pain and agony."

"I know from the Merciful Lord what you don't know," Prophet Jacob said wisely. "I'll go back to my room now till it's time to break my fast. If you let my grandchild bring me the food he prepared for me, I'd be very grateful."

Later that evening, the ten sons arrived weary and anxious to see their families. The eldest son hadn't been home in a long time, and after greeting his sons and wife outside, he asked about his father before going to see him in his room.

"How is he doing?" Reuben asked hopefully.

"I don't know," the woman replied, "he pretty much kept to himself all that time, except this morning he came out of his room smiling, saying he could smell Joseph in the air. Honestly, I think he's lost in his love for him!"

"Hey! That's my father you're talking about. And the Great Lord's prophet!" her husband scolded her. "What else did he say?"

"Nothing." The woman was ashamed of herself for insulting the prophet. "He just smiled and said there's a lot we don't know."

"Did he mention anything about a shirt?" the eldest brother asked.

"No, not that I know of." The woman was confused. "What shirt?"

There was no time to explain. Jacob had a beautiful mysterious connection with his beloved Joseph, and from his sudden change of feelings, it was obvious he smelt his scent from miles and miles away. The eldest son was filled with hope and admiration of how sensational people of faith could be. His father didn't need to see evidence; he just relied on his pure feelings and the energies of his beautiful soul. Reuben ran to his father's room with Joseph's shirt and just barged in, impatient to obey his young brother's request to cast it on Prophet Jacob's face.

"Forgive me for charging in unannounced, father," he apologised as he went down on his knees to kiss Jacob's hand, "but I couldn't wait to see you."

"Thanks to the Great Lord for your safety, son," Jacob patted his head warmly, still smiling at Joseph's scent that now filled the whole room. "I hope your trip was rewarding."

"It really was…" Reuben wept softly. Coming face to face with his father's blindness was far harsher than hearing about it. His hands were shaking with old age and weakness, and his white, swollen eyes seemed to be engraved with tears. Before Jacob could ask any more questions about his sons, Reuben softly covered his face with Joseph's shirt, feeling his heart about to stop with hopeful anticipation.

Jacob gasped when he felt the cloth cover his face; he then held it with both hands and breathed its scent in deeply, breaking down in tears of joy and relief. All his family gathered around silently to witness this moment, sobbing regretfully at the heartache they'd caused their dear father. Once upon a time they handed him a shirt that belonged to Joseph, triggering a burning agony they thought would never be extinguished. And tonight, after decades of grief, a shirt that belonged to Joseph soothed his throbbing pain, as they listened to him praise the Lord over and over again.

"Where did you get this?" he asked in utter shock.

"Joseph gave it to me. We finally found him, father."

"Joseph gave this to you?"

"Yes, he said it would heal your eyes."

"Joseph is alive! I knew it in my heart all this time. The Lord never lets His believers down, never. Joseph is alive!" Jacob wept happily.

"Yes, he is, father," Judah admitted, searching his father's face for a sign his eyesight had been restored. "He's the same fair minister we've been going to see in Egypt all this time."

"Thanks to the Great Lord!" Jacob lifted his head up to the sky with a smile. "What about Benjamin?" he then asked, reaching his hand out to pat Reuben on the shoulder.

"Benjamin lives in the same palace with Joseph. You were right, father! Your son never stole. He's an honourable man, and he's become Joseph's right-hand man. They're royalty now and they serve people with justice and kindness. I wish…" he put his head down, crying hysterically, "I wish you could see with your own eyes how truly successful and prosperous they've become."

Jacob lifted his son's chin up and softly wiped his tears. He then helped his son up, and straightened out his crumpled shirt with his palms lovingly. "Then take me to see them, dear son," he smiled.

"Father…?" Reuben tried to control his emotions, studying the look on his father's face.

"You need to comb this beard. No son of a prophet wanders around untidy and ruffled this way." Jacob crossed his arms, scolding him with a gentle smile.

"You can see me?" Reuben gasped for air, feeling the relief and joy would soon cause his heart to collapse.

"Thanks to the Merciful Lord, I can see you all now, but sadly I cannot bring myself to look at you. Why? Why, sons of Jacob? Why didn't you tell the truth and save me from decades of sorrow?"

"Forgive us, father," they all went down to the floor to kiss their father's feet. "Ask the Lord to forgive our sins, father! We have caused you and our brothers so much pain. Forgive us, please."

"How many times did I ask you to tell me what really happened to Joseph? How many times did I tell you to ask God for forgiveness?"

"We were scared of your reaction and so very ashamed of what we had done."

"Joseph has forgiven us, father! Ask him, he really has."

"If you too do not forgive us, we are doomed, prophet of God. Have mercy on your own flesh and blood."

"I will ask my Lord to forgive you all. He is the Oft-Forgiving and the Most Merciful," Prophet Jacob said sadly.

He hugged his eldest son warmly and then the rest of his sons ran to him like thirsty, drained men running away from fire, finding a bountiful well full of pure, resurrecting water in his embrace. They all hugged their father and wept in his arms, like little boys reunited with their parents after being lost in the cruel wilderness for so long. The nightmare was finally over, and for the first time in more than thirty years, the ten men had a soundless, peaceful sleep.

Packing their belongings didn't take much effort from the women, since they hardly owned anything to begin with. Most of their furniture and clothes had been sold in exchange for money or food during the drought years, but despite poverty and death surrounding the city, Jacob's house was brought back to life with a calm, soothing tide of tranquillity. The ten sons were finally freed from their suffocating chains of jealousy and guilt, blooming gradually with an appreciative sense of bliss. Prophet Jacob's smile trailed heavenly drops of joyful gratitude down the tracks of their journey to Egypt. He looked twenty years younger as he sat in the caravan with his grandchildren, telling them stories about their uncle Joseph whom they were soon going to meet. The desert sand gleamed with a golden reflection, and the cold hearts that once plotted evil plans melted in the heat of the sun as they all turned a new page in their lives.

"The messengers reported back, your Excellency," one of the guards addressed Joseph, who sat with his brother Benjamin on the terrace waiting patiently for news. "A flock of a prophet's family coming from Palestine just passed through the country's main gates."

Joseph jumped up quickly, knocking down the silver food tray one of the servants was just about to set down on the serving table.

"I'm so sorry," Joseph apologised, helping her clean the mess on the floor. "Please forgive me, I just couldn't contain myself."

"Is that the family you told us about, your Excellency?" the old woman looked at him with compassion.

"Yes, they're finally here," he said excitedly. He looked back at his young brother lovingly, with tears of joy filling his eyes.

"Go see them, son! I'll prepare the best dinner Egypt has ever seen for all of you." She patted his shoulder warmly.

"Thank you," Joseph said politely, before hurrying outside with Benjamin to greet his parents and family.

Their strong Arabian horses raced with their pounding hearts across the city to the main gates, taking Joseph and Benjamin to where the awaited caravan was stopping. Joseph dismounted his horse, unaware of people's admiring stares and flattering comments. His heart pulled him like a magnet to the camel that carried his parents, and he rushed to embrace them with so many unspoken words and a stream of longing tears. His father held Joseph's face between his shaking palms, staring at his beauty, scared to even blink and miss out on the glory of this fascinating moment. Total strangers stared at the minister crying in his parent's arms and they all wept softly, touched by the closeness the prophet and his son shared and the love they cherished in their hearts. The brothers gathered around them, protective and appreciative of their bond for the very first time in their lives. It was the happiest moment they had experienced by far, and they took turns to hug Joseph and Benjamin warmly, thankful their family had been finally reunited again.

"You haven't changed, Joseph," Jacob said lovingly. "You're still as handsome and dignified as I have always remembered you."

"I can't find the words to describe how much I've missed you, my dear beloved father," Joseph wept. "Please forgive me if I have caused you any pain."

"I don't remember being in any pain," Jacob smiled, holding on tight to his son's hand, afraid to let go and lose him again. "The Lord has brought you back to me, my son. I feel nothing but blissful joy. May the Lord always grant us His Mercy and blessings."

"Attention everyone!" Joseph lifted his hand, addressing the gathered crowd. "This is Prophet Jacob, the Lord's noble prophet, and his wife and sons. This is my family that I've longed to reunite with for more than thirty years. With the king's permission, I hope you will welcome them into your country like you have welcomed and embraced me." He then put his hand on his elder brother's shoulder. "These men are my dear brothers and without them I wouldn't be here now. I owe my whole life to this beautiful blessed family, and it would bring so much happiness to my heart if you all accept them here with us in Egypt, one of the greatest Arab nations."

The crowd cheered agreeably at their respected minister's request, and made way for the caravan to move forward to the palace. Joseph carried his father and put him on top of the camel's back, then held its rein and walked proudly beside it through the applauding crowd. His whole family followed, amused at the splendid welcome, happily greeting people with gratitude and pleasure, till they finally arrived at the palace. Joseph raised his parents to the throne where they were greeted by the king of Egypt himself. His father's face was bright like the sun; beaming with faith, strength and knowledge. His stepmother glowed like the moon, with a shimmering light of compassion and tenderness. His eleven brothers glimmered like celestial planets; each unique in his own special way and yet all huddled together around the sun and moon, absorbing the light of their wisdom and devotion. It was a picturesque scene of magnificent glory that Joseph stared back at, mesmerised in complete and utter awe...

The king of Egypt gave a heartwarming speech about Joseph's contributions and achievements in the years of famine, and praised his noble traits and righteousness. Prophet Jacob was beyond proud of his son. He and Leya stepped down to join his other sons and then they all bowed respectfully to Joseph before falling down in prostration in gratefulness to the One and Only Lord.

Joseph stepped down and kneeled closer to Jacob. "Oh my father, this is the interpretation of my dream!" he exclaimed, his eyes shining the same way they did when he was a little excited child. "My Lord has made the vision I saw years ago come true. My Lord has been kind to me, father. He took me out of prison and brought you out of the bedouin life here to Egypt after the devil came between my brothers and me. How can I ever show my gratitude to Him? Truly my Lord is the Most Kind and the Most Wise!"

Joseph picked his words as carefully and lovingly as a wise farmer picked ripe fruits. Even though he suffered in the well more than he did in prison, he chose not to mention that, lest he hurt his brothers' feelings or turn his father against them. He chose forgiveness over revenge, family over triumph, and love over hatred and blame.

Prophet Jacob gazed at his beloved son with eyes full of admiration and respect. He was a true, golden symbol of genuine faith and wisdom. He was the echoing voice of a religion based on compassion and concern for other people's welfare, a solid conviction that the Glorious Exalted Lord is our only Guardian, and in Him we put our full trust and faith. From being oppressed by his brothers, thrown away, enslaved, enticed, falsely convicted and then unjustly imprisoned, Joseph's life events could have turned him into a bitter man seeking vengeance. But then again, his amazing character did not just haphazardly emerge from nowhere; his difficulties had given him a sense of appreciation and a special understanding of life. It filled him with gentleness and a unique awareness of life's different perspectives...

Joseph walked alone outside the palace into the open terrace, closed his eyes and threw his head back. He put his palm out and felt the little droplets of rain drizzle on his hand. He smiled a knowing smile worth a million words...

No matter how hard life gets and how dark the world seems, sadness never lasts, and the truth will always prevail...

Just remember to never forget how strong you are...

And that one day your dreams can and will come true...

One day...

Milton Keynes UK
Ingram Content Group UK Ltd.
UKHW030746221024
449869UK00001B/29